Ladies of Letters Log On

Ladies of Letters
Log On

Carole Hayman and Lou Wakefield

A *Time Warner* Paperback

First published in Great Britain as a paperback
original in 2002 by Time Warner Paperbacks

Copyright © Carole Hayman and Lou Wakefield 2002

The moral right of the authors has been asserted.

A CIP catalogue record for this book
is available from the British Library.

ISBN 0 7515 3219 3

Typeset in Berkeley by M Rules
Printed and bound in Great Britain by
Clays Ltd, St Ives plc

Time Warner Paperbacks
An imprint of
Time Warner Books UK
Brettenham House
Lancaster Place
London WC2E 7EN

www.TimeWarnerBooks.co.uk

Le CLINIC de APHRODITE
Faxos
Greece

1st October 2001

Dear Lou and Carole,

Yes, I'm still here. And, can you believe it, I'm still wearing the bandages. As you will recall the first facelift went horribly wrong, as did the second, third and fourth. I have no idea what or whom I will look like when I'm finally unwrapped on Thursday next week. My daughters will be present; they are bringing with them a bottle of champagne. Though I fear cyanide may turn out to be my drink of choice.

A highlight of my stay here has been reading "Ladies of Letters Log On". The manuscript had to be smuggled in as laughter is strictly forbidden during the post-operative period. According to my surgeon, Dr Elias Poppolonika, "Thas 'ow Mrs Blair got 'er mouth, she was healing good until she stretched her lips laughing at some stupid English joke." I pray the same fate has not befallen me because I was unable to contain myself whilst reading the e-mails passing between Vera and Irene.

As you know my own family life is somewhat

baroque: I still can't understand what my eldest daughter sees in Nikita, the four-foot-seven white-faced clown she married last year. I curse the day the Moscow State Circus pitched its tent on the recreation ground in Leicester. However, my own family excesses pale into insignificance when compared to those of Irene and Vera's families.

Thursday

The bandages came off at midday. I could not bring myself to look in the mirror that Dr Poppolonika held up before me. The expression on my youngest daughter's face spoke volumes; it reminded me of the time she trod in a dog turd whilst running barefoot in the park.

This afternoon I sat on the balcony of my room, which overlooks the busy market square. Within minutes a pointing crowd had gathered below. Old women crossed themselves and muttered prayers. Somebody in the throng whispered, "Frankenstein." I may need a sixth operation.

My daughters have returned to their homes in, respectively, Moscow and Leicester. I owe Dr Poppolonika many millions of drachmas. Drachmas I do not have. God knows I am not a litigious woman – since Leicester City Council took *me* to court for stumbling over and cracking one of the paving slabs, I have tried to steer clear of the law. However, in desperation I may be forced to sue your publishers for actual bodily harm, due to excessive laughter caused by me reading "Ladies of Letters Log On".

I have already procured the services of a dashing young lawyer, Spiro Thaddapopolis. He recently made legal history here after successfully defending an overworked donkey in court.

Things look bad. Please ask Vera and Irene to contact me at the above address. I need their invaluable wisdom and advice.

Yours with love,

Sue Townsend

PS I have just caught a glimpse of myself in the bathroom mirror. Consequently I am going under the knife again tomorrow. Pray for me.

42 The Limes,
Hethergreen

Dear Vera,

As per usual on a visit over here, you managed to leave behind most of what you brought with you. Ergo, laundered and enc. is your handkerchief, which I retrieved from behind the cushion of the settee; your almost empty-tube of denture fixative, which had somehow been trodden into the dining-room carpet; a book entitled "Families and How To Survive Them", which I can only assume is yours – you must tell me how it ends some time; a pair of fuschia tights, which I found *in* the lavatory cistern – goodness knows what you were up to, but I thought at the time you were making some pretty strange noises in there; and what appears on close examination to be a half-sucked gobstopper, but which on first viewing I mistook for an eyeball! Considering you only popped in for lunch, I think that this time you excelled yourself in the bits-dropping-off-you stakes.

It was lovely seeing your daughter Karen again, and so good of her to let you join us on the spur of the moment, on a date that had been in both our diaries for weeks. She seems reconciled now to her husband St John's extra-marital behaviour with your son Howard's surrogate baby's mother, and to the fact that her new niece or nephew, when it's born, will actually be her step-child. On second thoughts, perhaps the book on surviving families was hers, poor girl. Do give her my love, and tell her I'll be over for that weekend break just as soon as Beryl-next-door is out of hospital with her bottom.

Fond regards,

Irene

The Coach House
The Bothy
Little Shagthorne

Dear Irene,

Also "as per usual" the words "dog" and "manger" come to mind when replying to your last. I'm far too busy preparing for my Dales TV chat-show to take offence, but you should know that it was only on my persuasion that Karen came at all. She said she was tired and "couldn't be bothered" to drive all that way. Knowing how much you depend on the kindness of strangers and how disappointed you would be, I offered to drive her. Really, I wish I hadn't.

I'm aware that you believe in plain food but your "lunch" of stewed beef with prunes had the effect even several bowls of All-Bran can't achieve on my innards, hence my sojourn in the lavatory. Your cistern is faulty by the way, I could only get it to flush by tying my tights round the ballcock. Good job I always carry a spare pair. The "gob-stopper" is in fact an indigestion pill. I popped it into my mouth between courses. Unfortunately, to cap it all (or rather, to de-cap it) your syrup tart dislodged my dentures at first bite, hence the need for fixative. I wondered what had happened to the pill.

Both Karen and I were very disappointed not to have the promised introduction to your long-lost son Christopher. We speculated about it on the return journey and wondered, since you didn't mention him, whether you have already had one of your famous "fallings out". I actually left "Families and How To Survive Them" as a subtle hint. Pity you didn't take it. Naturally I wouldn't have said a word about any of this had your letter not all but demanded an explanation.

Must stop and get back to work on my new Dales TV morning-magazine chat-show. Did I mention that? It's to be entitled "Dales Diaries" and given the massive response in Great Shagthorne to my appearance in "A Life With Sheep", and their desperation for ratings, they plan to put me on the air very shortly.

Fond regards,

Vera

irene@thelimes.hethergreen.com

Dear Vera,

I shall pass over your obviously jealous remarks about my cooking, since Karen so clearly relished the lunch – she hugged me in the kitchen, in fact, between courses when she helped me out with the plates, and told me, with sentimental tears in her eyes, that she'd had nothing like it since school dinners. The dear girl. What does concern me, though, is that you said she "couldn't be bothered" to drive over to see me. I think I am secure enough in my relations with your lovely daughter to be certain that if she said that about coming here to see me, all cannot be well with her. Apathy, of course, is a classic symptom of depression, and it would be perfectly natural for any young woman in her position to feel depressed – three children, unfaithful husband, the strain of having her mother living in the marital home . . . Isn't Howard's surrogate baby's mother due to give birth at any moment? If I were you I would keep a very watchful eye on Karen over the next few weeks. I know that if I had had to witness a child of my late husband Clive's pop out of another woman, and had then to welcome it into the bosom of my family, I would have felt like doing something quite uncharacteristic and extremely giddy.

I'm sorry to disappoint you about my relations with my son Christopher, by the by, which are in the best of health, thank you so much for asking. He's coming over at the weekend, as a matter of fact, to take me out for a run in his Portia. Which puts me in mind of Shakespeare's old saying, Vera (I'm currently doing an evening class in literal appreciation and we've just dissected "The Merchant of Venice") – "The quality of mercy is not strainéd, It droppeth as the gentle rain from heaven upon the place beneath". Since you are "the place beneath" in this particular instance, I shall not strain my mercy either. You are forgiven for not reading the notice in my smallest room, "Please pull chain GENTLY". There would have been *years* more usage in my ballcock if you had followed this instruction to the letter.

All the best,

Irene

<u>vera@dalesdiaries.com</u>

Dear Irene,

As you'll see from the above, I've got a new address to accommodate the immense e-mail I anticipate from my emminent TV programme. Speaking of jealousy, I notice you make no mention of it in your last. Probably your memory isn't what it was (I'm sure you'll deny, for instance, that you had three sherries before lunch last week) so let me refresh it. "A Life With Sheep" was a wonderfully illuminating "tick on the wall" documentary made about all us Great Shaggers last year. My son Howard, his partner Antony and their attempts to get pregnant by surrogacy on their sheep farm were the original subjects, hence the title, but for some reason Dales TV decided I was the star and the public agreed with them. The producer, Benjy Hartley-Dixon, asked me if I would like to host (I suppose, really, that should be "hostess"!) my own chat-show and ever since then he and I have been working on what he calls "the format". It's been through forty-two drafts. I could do with Shakespeare's help myself, I'd no idea so much re-writing was involved in a simple chat-show. I imagined I'd just go in front of the cameras and *chat*!

The reason, by the way, for Karen's so-called

"depression" is that owing to the above I've had to give up (temporarily) being head cook and baby minder. For once in her life she's having to do it herself. The results, of course, are disastrous. It's hardly surprising St John "strayed" – a less generous husband would have left home entirely long since. The way to a man's heart is through his stomach, as you and I have always agreed, albeit we have differences over what's acceptable to that organ. Oops, doorbell . . .

It was Zizi, Tasmin and Polly, my "researchers". Their average age is sixteen so I don't know what they can know about life, but I hope their search for it has been fruitful – I'm exhausted!

All for now,

Vee

PS Sorry about your ballcock. I've never known one respond to handling "gently". I suppose that's the result of overuse. Perhaps by Beryl and her bottom?

howard&antony@sheepshag.com

Dear Rene,

Mumsie mentioned you'd been enquiring after our pregnancy, so I thought I'd grab a moment between sheep milking and yoghurt fermenting to let you know how we're doing.

Our surrogate mum, Natasha, or "Tash" as we call her, has settled into our community well. We've managed to wean her on to organic food and natural fibres and have all had a great time playing Abba to our unborn baby and reading it Harry Potter. Tash will shortly be having a home birth, with myself and Antony in attendance. There'll be an official midwife as well, though there's little that Ants and I don't know about delivery after breeding a pedigree sheep flock! We've made it up with brother-in-law, St John, and Tash's husband, Wayne, but sister Karen is still a problem. She's just so selfish. After all, St John was only trying to help by impregnating Tash, when the syringe method failed.

Our main worry is how we'll cope after the baby's born and Tash goes home. We were approached after "A Life With Sheep" to turn Sheepdipper's Shed into a theme farm, but the developers wanted to have Ants and I dressed up as "heritage" shepherds. I didn't mind that so much – I'm a natural for Little Bo Peep! – but I drew the line at all the additives they wanted to put in the yoghurt. Back to square one on the finances! We're now thinking of making a child-friendly, sheep-themed educational centre. With Karen and St John's three and our new baby, we'll soon have plenty of kids to entertain! You must come and visit after the birth and see our little one for yourself. We're so excited!

Loads of love,

Howie

irene@thelimes.hethergreen.com

Dear Vera,

If I've told you once I've told you a thousand times –
with Beryl's bottom it isn't a question of how much she
has to "go", it's a question of what's around it, in it, and
what comes out of it that's the problem. If you want
more details than that I'll give you her phone number –
she'll tell anyone chapter and verse of the sorry tale at
the drop of a hat.

All for now. I feel the Muse coming upon me.

Irene

PS Don't you think poor Karen has suffered enough
already, without her own Mother turning against her?

irene@thelimes.hethergreen.com

Dear Howard,

Thank you for your e-mail. I'm glad to hear things have settled down in your complex family relations, although I do think both you and your Mother are being rather harsh on poor Karen. Give her time – you can't expect her to be overjoyed at the fact that her husband was "intimate" with another woman, however well-meaning he thought he was being at the time. The fact of the matter is, in a few weeks she will be an aunt and a step-mother in one fell swoop. I know if it was me, it would take some digesting.

A propose of coming to grips with complicated situations, I was most struck by the idea that you are reading to the new baby through its Mummy's tummy, and I have taken the liberty of penning a few verses to explain to it its unusual situation, vis a vee its parentage. Perhaps you would be so kind as to read to it the following ode . . .

All good wishes, and love to Antony,

Rene

Welcome, New Baby Small

a poem
by
Irene Spencer

Hello in there, my little one, in all your unborn
    glory,
Quite soon you'll be out here with us, so you
    should know your story:
In common with all other babes, you'll pop out
    Mummy's tummy,
From whence you'll be in Daddy's arms, and that's
    where it gets funny –

Where other babies have one Dad, for you there
    will be four,
And Mums, that usually come in ones, you'll
    have – oh, two or more.
So let me introduce you now, to save a later
    muddle,
To all your parents – six in all – my, what a lot to
    cuddle!

There's Daddy St John (with long legs), a vet, who
    gave you life,

And Mummy Karen, who isn't your Mum, but is
   your Daddy's wife,
Then there's Daddy Wayne, of course, who
   wouldn't be a relation,
If he weren't married to Mummy Tash, who gave
   you your creation.

Last comes Daddy Howard and his partner Daddy
   Ants,
(You'll know them when you see them – they'll be
   the ones who change your pants).
You'll live happy ever after on their farm
   Sheepdipper's Shed,
And they will be your parents, even though they
   can't be wed.

Dear Rene,

Thanks for the hysterical poem! We read it out loud, screaming with laughter, and it obviously struck a chord with our little unborn, as he/she began to kick wildly. Poor Tash got quite bilious. She had to lie down and have one of Ants' famous massages. That's another money-spinner we've decided to try out at Sheepdipper's. Ants is wonderful with his hands, but there's only so much you can do to a sheep. His talents are rather wasted.

Your explanation of our baby's parentage did highlight a few bothersome areas. Calling it "Small" nearly provoked a climax! Ants and I have argued for months about what surname to give it. Naturally I favour Small and he favours Flowers. We've thought of a hyphen, but "Small-Flowers" sounds a bit . . . well, "lavender". Especially if it's a boy. We don't want to prejudice people's attitudes right from the beginning. As Mumsie keeps saying, "the poor little mite will have enough to contend with".

Big kisses,

Howie

PS Take your point about Karen. Perhaps we should ask her to be Godmother?

vera@dalesdiaries.com

Dear Irene,

Perhaps I should invite Beryl and her bottom on to my show? If what you say is true, she wouldn't be prone to awkward pauses. Send me her phone number and I'll pass it on to Zizi, Tasmin and Polly.

Vee

irene@thelimes.hethergreen.com

Dear Vera,

Had the most wonderful time with my son Christopher on Sunday. He picked me up in his Portia and drove me to a most exclusive restaurant over at Spittle Common, which is owned by a friend of his – you may have heard of him, given your interest in the culinary arts – Simon Strange? Has his own television show, "Strange Food", cooking for his friends at exclusive dinner parties – Chris has been on it several times, apparently. Attached is a photograph of the three of us, convivially post-pranial, which I thought you might like to see, given that you have all but suggested in the past that my good relationship with my son is a pigment of my imagination.

I had a word with Beryl-next-door, as you requested, about whether she'd be interested in baring all on your forthcoming cable-television programme, but she has declined. During this recent spell in the teaching hospital, she feels she has been "on show" enough – her bottom is so interesting to the medical establishment that it was taken to a laboratory to be professionally photographed for inclusion in a text book.

By the by, I hope you notice that I have "mentioned"

your television show, since you accused me in a recent e-mail of not alluring to it because of supposed jealousy. Honestly, Vera, sometimes I think you are still in a kind of school-playground-mentality mode with your accusations! Why on earth would I be jealous? As far as I'm concerned, I couldn't be more delighted that you have at last found a new hobby which satisfies the demands of your larger-than-life ego, and if you seriously think it could be otherwise then I am afraid you must be suffering from panaroeia. However, since we are on the subject, I would remind you that I still have an e-mail in my "inbox", sent by you last year, where you asked me to take part in the show as your co-presenter. I note that in the "not-mentioning-it" stakes, this subject has now become top of the league table.

All good wishes,

Irene

Dear Irene,

Yes, I have heard of Simon Strange. In fact I watched a few of his "dinner parties" and even tried one or two of the recipes. Strange food indeed. I hope he didn't serve you his stuffed squirrel. In my opinion, that would go better on a mantelpiece. His guests were pretty peculiar too. They were over-made-up, giggling wildly and waving their arms. And that was just the men. Quite honestly I wondered if they were "on something". Perhaps it was too much coriander. I don't recall seeing your son Christopher. But, of course, I didn't know him then. Nor do I now, for that matter. Anyway, I'm delighted that you all had such a good time. The wine, at least, must have been plentiful, judging by the photo I downloaded. Your eyes appear to be pointing in different directions.

Now, Irene. I've thought long and hard about whether to tell you this, but I've realised, after your recent incinerations, that it can't be avoided. It seems I was rather premature in offering to share my limelight with you. As a novice in the television world, I hadn't realised that no one pays any attention to what the "creatives" say and my pleas to include you as co-hostess have fallen on deaf ears. They insist they want someone charismatic. However, after seeing how handsome Christopher looks, specially in that lilac shirt, a brilliant idea has occurred to me. How about both of you coming on my first "Dales Diaries" TV programme and telling the story of how you lost him and then he found you? I'm sure it's sufficiently "shocking" and "revelatory" to fulfil the demands of my team of researchers. They are getting increasingly desperate, and are now suggesting I interview Ann Widdecombe. I shudder at the thought of what *she* might reveal!

Take as long as you like to think about it and let me know by tomorrow morning. Incidentally, I wouldn't dream of asking Beryl to bare her bottom on my show. It's intended to be family viewing.

Fond regards,

Vera

Dear Vera,

Excuse the tardiness of my reply, but I have been extremely busy. In fact, I was just sitting at my laptop to "log on" to you on Wednesday when the doorbell rang and my life became a giddy whirl of exciting activity. Christopher had arrived in a red Lamburgergini and was wanting me to come with him there and then for a spin. Little did I know when I grabbed my jacket and handbag that the "spin" wouldn't stop until we had crossed and re-crossed the White Cliffs of Dover and toured through half of Europe! We arrived back here at The Limes, exhausted but exhilarated, three days later. Everything that I needed, he just went out and bought! I've come back with two new frocks, an Eve Saint Lawrence suit, new shoes, new underwear . . . ! Sons are so much more impulsive than daughters, aren't they? I have only remade Chris's acquaintance for a few short months, and in that time he has arrived here in a Jaguar, a Mercedes Sports Coupé, last week's Portia, this week's Lamburgergini . . . Indeed, such is his passion for motor cars (and, dare I say it, for his Mum!) that while we were in Prague on Friday, he popped out to get the morning papers and came back having swapped his

Lamburgergini for a Ford Mondeo, saying that I would be much more comfortable in a saloon car for the return journey. The dear boy. He was absolutely right, of course – little sports cars are lovely to look at but very awkward for ladies to get in to and out of elegantly, and rather short on leg room. Of course, he is something of an expert on motor cars, what with having his own Pre-Owned Vehicle Reallocation Consultancy.

As the miles rolled by us, I put to him your request of our appearing together on your "show" and, as I thought, he was of the same mind as I myself on the subject – we have no desire for our moving and complex tale of Christopher's origins to become entertainment for the cable-television-viewing public of Great and Little Shagthorne, thank you so much. He and I are blissfully happy to have found each other again after four decades, but neither of us feel the need to shout it from the rooftops.

So, good luck with Ann Widdecombe!

All good wishes,

Irene

Dear Irene,

I was beginning to think the conundrome I'd set you was proving too much and I should have asked Christopher directly. So, as soon as you explained he was a second-hand car dealer, I looked him up in Yellow Pages under C. Thorogood and took the liberty of sending him a reminder of our previous encounter and a personal invitation to appear on my show. We're fine for the first one, by the way, in case you were worried that your refusal would cause me any anxiety. Zizi, Tasmin and Polly have found a body-builder who's had a sex change and is coming on with his tattooed ex-wife for a bout of mud wrestling. Whoops, nearly made a mistake in my haste and wrote "nude wrestling". Wouldn't want you to think we're just into sensationalism. Anyway, do let me know if you change your mind.

All for now,

Vera

vera@dalesdiaries.com

Dear Christopher,

I feel I can call you that, after our brief but entrancing former acquaintance. You may remember me as the lady you rescued from a building pit in my daughter's garden (now a luxurious swimming pool!). I'd had a bang on the head and was rather confused and when I saw your golden curls hovering over me, I asked if you were an "angel".

I don't know what your Mum has told you about me since, or if she's told you anything at all . . . sometimes Irene can be very possessive. She likes to keep her "relationships" in separate boxes. However, I recently sent her an invitation for you and her to appear on my "Dales Diaries" TV show. I needn't tell you what good publicity a morning-magazine programme can be for a business enterprenewer such as yourself. We'll be reaching a global audience, my researchers have recently been chasing stories as far away as the North Pole. Not that they'd have a lot of use for old bangers there, but I don't doubt with your good looks and charm you could sell one to a walrus! Also, and don't pass this on to your Mum, we're still looking for a vibrant, young co-presenter . . . I won't say any more, but if you're as photogenious as you seem, you could be just the ticket!

Warm regards,

Vera Small

Dear Vera,

Christopher has "forwarded" the e-mail you wrote to him on to me, and I have to say that I am shocked to my foundations. How could you even *think* of going behind my back to try to tempt my son into betraying me? Where ever did you get the idea that he would join forces with you while keeping me in the dark? Does our so-called "friendship" mean nothing to you? I'll tell you what I think:

A) That you haven't even mentioned me to your producer as a possible co-presenter of the wretched show because you fear I might outshine you, and –

B) That you have become foolishly and giddily intoxicated with Christopher's charm and good looks and have started to fantasise, erroniatiously, that some romantic relationship could develop between you along the lines of Richard and Judy.

Unless you can prove my theories groundless, please do not trouble yourself either to reply to this missive, or indeed to ever contact me again.

Yours, hurt, bruised, confused and desiccated,
One who has hitherto always thought of herself as your erstwhile friend,

Irene Spencer

vera@dalesdiaries.com

Irene!

As usual you have totally misunderstood my
motives. I thought I was doing Christopher a favour.
Come to that, I thought I was doing *you* one, if
you're expecting to carry on the expensive lifestyle to
which you are obviously becoming accustomed. The
idea that I would be harbouring romantic allusions
for a man half, or even three-quarters, my age – how
old exactly were you when you had him, by the
way? – is ridiculous! I knew that you would take my
offer the wrong way, hence my request to him to
keep it to himself. *I* am shocked he hasn't treated my
e-mail as confidential, nor been civil enough to reply.
Not the behaviour of the gentleman I remember!
Perhaps, in his search for love and acceptance, he has
allowed himself to fall too much under other
influences.

Since you are obviously consumed with envy and
smarting desperately at your rejection, I have begged
Dales TV to think again. Otherwise, I can see I shall
never hear the end of it. Or rather, I *will* hear the
end of it, in terms of our "relationship". I'm sure, in

your present hurt, bruised, confused and dessicated state, you won't believe anything *I* say, so I have asked Zizi, Tasmin and Polly to get in touch with you personally.

Yours,

Vera

Dales TV
Horse Tooth Rd
Saddlecombe
Nr Gt Shagthorne

Friday 13th

Dear Mrs. Spencer,

On behalf of Dales TV and our producer Benjy
Hartley-Dixon, we would like to extend to you the
offer to co-present a pilot episode of our new show
"Dales Diaries". This will be a fun mix of popular
social, cultural, culinary and humorous strands. Vera
has told us lots about you. But we're sure, with a little
adjustment, you'll fit in.

Do say yes! We start rehearsals on Tuesday at 10.30.

Cheers,

Zizi, Tasmin and Polly

irene@thelimes.hethergreen.com

Monday

Dear Vera,

Thank you for your apology, which is duly accepted. I have just received by post – or "snail-mail" as we e-mailers now call it – the invitation to co-host "Dales Diaries", which, since you seem to be in an absolute last-minute pickle, I shall graciously accept. Since your "researchers" have not included their e-mail address, would you please be so good as to print off and deliver the following missive, and tell them I will be late for "rehearsals", as the first train to Little Shagthorne doesn't arrive till 11.30. I assume they will meet my expenses in full, so I shall take a cab when I get to the other end. I imagine that you mean me to stay with you while I am doing the show. Fortunately Beryl-next-door has been returned to the community by the hospital, so I'll ask her to do my lights and curtains until further notice.

Best wishes,

Irene

42 The Limes
Hethergreen

Dear Zizi, Tasmin and Polly,

Thank you for your invitation to co-present the
"Dales Diaries" cable-television show, albeit at short
notice. Since you do not mention renumeration in
your letter, please note that you will be contacted by
Mr Christopher Thorogood in due course, who is my
agent in these affairs.

I don't know if Vera has mentioned my proclivities
with the pen, but I am in fact something of a poet, and
as such will be able to contribute verse to suit most
occasions. I shall hope to be visited by the Muse
between now and when we meet tomorrow, and shall
surprise you accordingly.

Looking forward to the start of a fruitful and happy
relationship with you all.

Yours very sincerely,

Irene Spencer (Mrs)

<u>vera@dalesdiaries.com</u>

Tuesday 2.00 a.m.

Irene,

For goodness sake don't come! Just got in from a terrible row at Dales TV. My researchers Zizi, Tasmin and Polly have been sacked. Apparently, they didn't consult the producer Benjy Hartley-Dixon over your appointment. I've never heard language like it! He stormed round the studio like a toddler in a tantrum. Also discovered a problem with the budget. There isn't one.

Do hope you check your e-mail, before laying out on the train fare!

Vee

irene@thelimes.hethergreen.com

Tuesday night

Dear Christopher,

Well! Absolute mayhem here! But then, what else would I expect from anything that Vera tried to organise? Arrived at Great Shagthorne after a nightmare journey on the "train" – I use the inverted commas advisedly as most of the trip was spent on buses, being ferried between the railway stations that were closed for renovations. If I entrained and disentrained once, I did it a dozen times. Needless to say I was in a terrible state of anxiety by the time I reported for "rehearsals" three hours late, but that was as nothing compared to how I felt when I was greeted by the director, Benjy Hartless-Dixon and informed that I had been sacked before I had begun!

It transpires that Vera did e-mail me in the middle of last night to tell me not to come – but honestly! Who checks their e-mail at 3.00 a.m.? Certainly not I. Anyway, it's all been a storm in a teacup and I soon got order restored. Benjy's nose had been put out of joint because he felt he hadn't been consulted about my appointment, but as soon as he saw how "presentable" I was, and I showed him the poem I had written for inclusion in the first show, he immediately saw what a mistake he was making and hired me on the spot! I say "hired" – apparently he is expecting us to give our services for free initially, until we are the huge success that he is sure we will prove to be. I told him you would be ringing him to discuss this – at least I should be paid for my odes, surely?

I am currently staying with Vera's daughter Karen and her veterinarian husband St John, but I don't know how long that will last – Vera comes as part of the package, and we've already had "words". If it becomes unendurable I can always go and bunk up with her son Howard and his partner Antony, who in any case are soon expecting their first baby and might be grateful to have an experienced mother on hand to show them which way is up!

All my love, my little one,

Your loving Mummy,

Irene xxxxxxxxx and one for luck x

Welcome, Dear Viewer

a poem
by
Irene Spencer

Imagine, as you're sitting there,
Upon your sofa, or your chair,
That we are not some remote stars,
Who travel the world in chauffeured cars.
No – think of us as your old friends,
Who've just popped in to make amends
For any hardship in your life –
Whatever troubles, whatever strife
You may have suffered, we are here,
To comfort you and give you cheer.

My name is Irene – hers is Vera,
And to us you couldn't be dearer,
Or more treasured in our hearts,
As you watch us take our parts.
Now, just pretend that your TV,
Is a two-way mirror and we see
You clear as day – is this not fun?
The grey skies clear, out comes the sun!
So just remember, no more sorrow –
We're here today, and every morrow!

vera@dalesdiaries.com

Wed. 3.30 a.m.

Dearest Howard (and Antony),

I really hate to have to make this request, but I don't know where else to turn. To put it bluntly, can Irene come and stay with you at Sheepdipper's Shed for the foreseeable future? Now, before you make the inevitable response (I can almost hear the groans!) let me just say that if you refuse, your only Mother's life will become a living Hell and she may, in a moment of agony, take the only way out, and end it. I don't want to over-dramatise – Goodness knows I have been accused of that often enough by Karen to have learned my lesson – but Irene has been here for less than a day and has already managed to create chaos.

Having been apprised by me, in plenty of time, that her services were no longer required by Dales TV, she wilfully ignored my warning – as usual I was trying to let her down gently – and turned up at the studio, wearing full-length satin that looked like a nightgown, a beaded Pashmina (a present from her son Christopher, so she said!), a new hair rinse (lilac) and make-up that her salon "facial artiste" had copied from a photo of Joan Collins. I ask you! For a warm and informal morning chat-show! To add insult to outrage, she'd come prepared with what she called an "Opening Ode" which she insisted on reading. I thought the producer, Benjy Hartley-Dixon, was going to defenestrate there and then. Fortunately, he wears baggy corduroys and I managed to catch him by the seat as he climbed on to the window sill. He said he was trying to swat a bluebottle, but I've read all about stressed executives throwing themselves from skyscrapers. In this case we were on the ground floor (Dales TV can't afford a skyscraper), but it just shows poor Benjy's desperation! Of course, he had to give her the job, what else could he do? My dear little researchers, Zizi, Tasmin and Polly, have also been reinstated. Quite honestly, who else were they going to get to put up with such a ridiculous situation?

Irene was wreathed in smiles of triumph and to cap it all, seems to assume she can stay here for the duration. She's sleeping in Karen's turret, and I've already had to climb the wretched ladder with Horlicks, haemorrhoid cream and a hot water bottle, as Karen refuses to let her come down. I can't endure weeks of her blaming me and sulking. Karen that is, not Irene. Although, come to think of it, the same could apply. The final straw was Irene's demand for "Roger's Thesorus" for help in "creating" another poem! I said we had no one by the name of Roger living at The Bothy and reminded her, in no uncertain terms, that as well as the notoriously treacherous ladder, there are one hundred and twenty stairs up to the turret!

Dearest, darling, Howie – and of course, Antony – please, PLEASE, save me and the rest of your suffering family!

Mumsie xxxxxx

howard&antony@sheepshag.com

Dear Irene,

We wondered if you'd like to stay here while you're "recording" "Dales Diaries"? Don't give putting us out a thought. We could do with another pair of hands – to say nothing of the rest of the body. Speaking for ourselves, we're finding this pregnancy exhausting!

Between you and us, Mumsie's explained that there are a few problems over at The Bothy, so let us know when you want your stuff collecting and we'll drive over in the yoghurt delivery van.

Look forward to seeing you,

Howard and Antony

irene@thelimes.hethergreen.com

Dear Howard and Antony,

Thank you for your invitation to stay with you, but I'm afraid I must decline. I know you need me to help with the impending baby, but your sister Karen needs me to be here with her as she is not getting on at all well with your Mother at the moment, and I am having to act as an emoillient on troubled waters. Once I have got this situation here on an even keel, I will of course be delighted to come and stay with you to lend a hand.

All fond wishes to you both,

Irene x

irene@thelimes.hethergreen.com

Dear Howard and Antony,

Please ignore my e-mail of an hour ago, and come and collect me from your Mother's as soon as possible. Naturally Karen is very disappointed at my change of heart, but she will cope. If I stay here a moment longer I fear for my continued working relationship with your Mother, not to mention my life – she has started hurling objects at me now, and I am nursing a very nasty bruised foot as a result! Currently we are not speaking, and are therefore having to communicate by handwritten notes.

See you soon, I hope.

All love,

Rene

Vera,

Have gone to stay with Howard and Antony. Will see you at the "Dales Diaries" "rehearsals" in the morning, by which time I hope you will be feeling somewhat calmer.

Irene

PS Have tried to glue your ormolu clock back together again, but there appear to be a few pieces left over which don't seem to fit anywhere.

PPS Am taking the cold compress with me. Will return it tomorrow.

Howard,

For Chrissakes keep the barmy old bat for as long as poss. I was about to brain her. Our dear mother had already had one go at it! As if having *her* around full-time wasn't enough! Sorry to lumber you, but after all, you do owe me one. What goes around, etc. etc.

Karen

vera@dalesdiaries.com

Dearest Howard,

So sorry about the confusion! Irene simply refused to leave, even after your generous invitation. Not satisfied with having me struggling up and down to the turret every five minutes, the final nail was her refusing to stay in it and stalking down (uninvited) to my kitchen. There am I, happily trying out an *inspired* recipe for banana chutney (enc-ed) to include in my organural TV show, when Irene appears like a polter-giced over my shoulder and, with her usual carelessness of other people's feelings, remarks that she "doesn't think it will televise well, as it is the colour of vomit". I was so incensed I dropped the dratted banana skin, skidded on it, crashed into the Welsh dresser, dislodged my favourite "antique" ormolu clock, which shot off the shelf and hit Irene on the foot before falling on to the quarry-tiled floor (I rue the day I had that laid) and smashing into a million pieces. I'm so upset. That clock has been in the family since my daytrip to Italy last summer. It will never be any use (as a clock) again.

Of course, Irene made a tremendous fuss, hopping about and yelling as though she'd been attacked by an axe murderer. St John rushed in to see what had happened. Sabrina, Nelson and little Millie were all in tears of fright and Karen was threatening to walk out completely. St John immediately applied a cold compress and gave Irene, at her insistence, a tetanus injection – something to do with the clock having come from Venice. (Oh, it is a relief to have a man with a syringe on tap. But I needn't tell *you* two that!) After that, even someone as pigheaded as Irene knew her welcome was out-stayed, hence the frantic e-mails.

Try and be patient and bear it for me. When I become a household name, I will make sure you and Antony are thoroughly remunerated.

Your suffering Mumsie xx

<u>Banana Chutney</u>
2 old bananas
1 half-baked apple
2 spring onions
1 clove garlic
Handful sultanas
Dollop of tarragon vinegar

Put all ingreeds except sultanas in blender. Whizz for 30 secs then mix in sultanas. Cool in fridge for an hour before use. Delicious with pork (or lamb!) kebabs.

irene@thelimes.hethergreen.com

Dearest Christopher,

These days my e-mail address seems very
inopposite, since I am not in Hethergreen at all, but
touring round the whole of Shagthorne, both Little and
Great! As I feared, Vera turned nasty almost before I'd
unpacked my bags at her daughter's sixteen-room
Georgian mansion house. You'd think Vera owned it,
rather than her delightful veterinarian son-in-law St
John, the way she bosses everybody around – she had
me locked in a turret in the West Wing, and even went
so far as to take away the ladder that connects it to the
rest of the house! In the end I was forced to tie some
sheets together to make my escape – I was dying for a
tinkle and there's no "on suite" up there – but
fortunately Vera's granddaughter Sabrina was passing
by below, and put the ladder back in place. She's a very
sweet little girl, and would be so pretty if she wore a
skirt and grew her hair.

I won't worry you with the full details of what
transpired when I "dared" to go into the kitchen after
visiting the bathroom. Suffice it to say that I am now
staying with Vera's gay son Howard and his partner
Antony at their farm, Sheepdipper's Shed, and am
nursing a gashed and bruised foot as a consequence of

Vera "going ballistic", as Sabrina would say. Fortunately, St John is medically trained, albeit on animals, so I was well cared for. And Howard and Antony are such dears they won't hear of me doing anything, so I'm a lady of leisure here on the farm.

Am rather anxious about "rehearsals" tomorrow though. Needless to say, Vera and I aren't speaking "off-camera", so I am forced to communicate with her via the written word. If you're free at the weekend, shall we go on another trip? I think I will be dying to get away by then to spend some time in "civilised" company.

Let me know, my little cherub.

Your loving Mummy,

Irene xxx ooo

dalesdiaries@dalestv.co.uk

Howard,

We go out live with our first "Dales Diaries" show
tomorrow morning! We've had so many teething
problems – literally. Irene has ordered new dentures,
which have failed to arrive. She will, needless to say, go
to any lengths to grab attention. There hasn't been time
to think about an audience. Can you and Antony and
Natasha come and be it? There is a small amount of
"studio participation", food tasting etc. That reminds
me, can you bring eight gallons of sheep's yoghurt with
you?

Oh. Must stop and find my notepad. Irene has just
waltzed into the "production office" to display her
"costume". We are not speaking at the moment, and
are "communicating" by memo.

Love,

Mumsie xx

Irene,

That shade makes your face look like an old cigar.
Besides, you will clash with me.

Vera

Vera,

My costume choice has had producer approval. Please go through Mr Benjy Hartless-Dixon if you want to make comments of a dolourterious nature.

Irene

Benjy!

Please make it clear to Irene she can't wear a trouser suit in luminescent puce. She seems to have forgotten _I_ am the "colourful" character.

Don't say I didn't warn you.

Vee

Vera,

Why are you passing handwritten
notes to <u>m e</u> – I thought it was just Irene
you weren't speaking to? While we're
on the subject, can you please bear in
mind that Dales TV is not at home to
Mrs Crosspatch or Madam Mardy, so will
both of you please try to act your age!

Best,

Benjy

Dear Benjy,

I will act my age if you will act yours. In my opinion, senior citizens are due respect from twenty-five-year-olds!

Best,

Vera

irene@thelimes.hethergreen.com

Dearest Christopher,

Thank goodness you found me again after all these
years – I really don't know what I'd have done, under
current circumstances, without a son to turn to. Today
Vera became so objectionable to me that even the
producer told her to grow up – and he's only in his
twenties, the poor lad! I won't go into the catalogue of
catastrophes we have been having here today, on this,
the eve of our little programme going "on air" to the
cable-television-viewing public of Little and Great
Shagthorne. Suffice it to say that Vera has plumbed
new depths of unpleasantness: hiding my dentures,
sending away the minicab driver who was couriering
an emergency new set I had ordered, pouring cold
water on the Eve Saint Lawrence trouser suit you
bought me in Prague, sniggering while I was
rehearsing the reading of my poem . . . I could go on,
but what would be the point? Jealous is jealous, no
matter how many words one might try to wrap it up
in. Perhaps if I had proved to be less of "a natural" in
front of the cameras, or if I weren't quite so
photogenic, or so popular with the "crew" – none of
which I can *help*, after all's said and done! – perhaps
then she would be happier. As it is, I just try to soldier

on as cheerfully as I can, replying as politely as possible to her copious handwritten notes which she thrusts at me every few minutes, despite her having been told in no uncertain terms by Benjy that he will not *tolerate* distention in his workforce.

Anyway, enough of that. It's already the early hours of the morning and I must try to get my beauty sleep for tomorrow's show. I've already tried and tried to get to sleep, but I'm too excited, and my fertile brain is bulging with new ideas for future programmes, new odes are queuing up impatiently to slither down my writing arm and on to virgin pages and, as if that were not enough for a retired woman my age, my mind keeps circling round the subject of *you*, my dearest, most cherished first-born, and how we came to be so cruelly parted, and so rapturously rejoined. I have told you my part of the story – how, as a young inexperienced girl I was ravaged by a so-called "friend" of my parents and frightened by him into keeping quiet about it, how I was cruelly criticised by my mother over the ensuing months for putting on so much weight, and of how you arrived, out of the blue it seemed, while I was blacking the grates that fateful Monday morning. I recounted how you were taken from my side and hurriedly given to a member of my father's church who knew a man who knew a woman who knew a couple who couldn't have children, and of how, though I begged and pleaded on my bended knees, I could get no information as to where you'd gone and was told to forget you.

What I long to know is all about your early years. I feel that I have missed out on the joy of a thousand small details of your life – your first word, your first day at school, the drawings and paintings and models you would have carried home in your little ink-stained hand, whether you passed the eleven plus, did you join the Boy Scouts and, if so, what badges did you attain, etc. etc. *ad nausea*. When we go out together at the weekend, will you tell me more? And are there photographs you could bring to show me? Being reunited with you after four decades is such a miracle that sometimes, when I'm writing to you, or sitting next to you in one of your motor cars, I literally have to pinch myself to see if I am truly awake.

Speaking of which, finally I suddenly feel thoroughly exhausted and must retire to my bed. To sleep – perchance to dream of you, my dearest, sweetest son, and now, no longer a yearning, aching dream of despair, but a dream of happiness, of fulfillment, of being made whole!

Tomorrow is a huge day in the humble history of I, Irene Spencer, whom fate has decreed to be plucked from obesity and hurled into the glare of televised "stardom", but it is as nothing, believe me, compared to knowing that in a few short days I will be by your side again, Mother and son, conjoined in an ecstatic symphony concerto of maternal bliss.

Till Saturday, then. God speed these hours. As I write, I brush away soft tears of joy which trickle their trail o'er these happy cheeks.

Your adoring, loving, doting,

Mummy Irene xxx

PS Forgot to mention – thanks so much for sending Roger's thesorus.

Dearest Howard,

Can't sleep . . . partly nerves and partly the jumbo
rollers with which Candy, our make-up girl, has set my
hair. Every time I try to lie down, my head rebounds
off the pillow. I had no idea those smiling presenters
had to endure so much torture! Talking of which, this
is by way of saying how grateful I am for your support
at this traumatic time. I'm so glad you and Antony and
Natasha will be there tomorrow to cheer me on . . .
don't be late, dear, will you? The show goes out
prompt at 10.30 and do wear something eye-catching.
The camera will be on you. And only you, apparently.
Your brother-in-law St John is of course working. Little
Sabrina will be at school and your sister Karen says she
is too "depressed" to come. How St John puts up with
her I will never know. I wish to goodness she'd get on
that Prozack. Of course a lot of it is jealousy of me. She
can't bear the fact that a woman of my years is still
attractive and desirable (if the cameraman's winks are
anything to go by!) and is about to become loved by
millions. Well, hundreds anyway.

It seems that Irene's "perfect" son Christopher won't
be attending, either. This is extremely odd as she has
been boring everyone rigid all week with stories of

how he "pampers" and "cherishes" her and is constantly whipping out the one photo she has of him and poking it under people's noses. If I hadn't seen him myself – once, and that in peculiar circumstances – I would be beginning to wonder whether he exists at all!

I'm afraid she's riding for a fall. She gets so over-emotionally wound up and then terribly let down. I needn't remind you of the way she was dumped by that rotter Bill Snapes, after all his empty promises. Even then she blamed me and said I'd deliberately come between them. She's as bad as Karen in the jealousy department. She's already attempted to drive a wedge between me and the producer, Benjy Hartley-Dixon, and she'd win Olympic gold if they included a competition for space invasion! As soon as that little red light goes on above the camera (there is only one, unfortunately) she leaps in front of it, ogling and gurning. She waves her arms about so much Benjy asked her if she'd taken a course in sign language! She's been so offensive, I couldn't trust myself to speak to her and have had to resort to note-giving. Poor little Zizi, Tasmin and Polly have been run off their feet passing scraps of paper between us. They look close to nervous breakdown. Hardly surprising when you consider that with all the overtime (unpaid), they are working for less than the national minimum wage. And there was me under the misaprobriation that jobs in the "medium" were so well-remunerated. But then, of course, they are only children.

Well, dear, must finish and try to get some shut-eye, albeit in an upright position. I'm sure I'll be fine. I am what is known in the business – so Zizi tells me – as a "trooper". I just hope Irene can take the strain. But, I suppose, as per, I'll be around to pick up the pieces.

'Til I see your smiling faces the other side of the camera.

Bless you,

Mumsie

Vera,

　　To you this humble card I send,
　To jog your mind that I'm your <u>friend</u>,
　Good luck this morn, and "break a leg",
　And try to be civilised, please, I beg,
　For we're on show before the nation –
　Let's make it a cause for celebration!

With all good wishes for the making of our first "Dales Diaries".

Your co-presenter,

Irene

PS Don't forget to step back and to your LEFT after your intro to my poem, and don't fling out your arm – I'm JUST behind you. We don't want a repeat of rehearsals!

Irene,

Thank you for your apology. I will take the advice to "break a leg" in the spirit in which, I'm sure, it was intended. Though frankly, in those ridiculous high-heeled boots you're wearing, I think it's more likely to be you. I'm glad you have reminded us that it is "friendship" that has brought us to this exalted position. Particularly mine for you. Anyway, good luck and DO KEEP STILL. Remember what Benjy said about wild gestures giving the viewers migraine.

Yours,

Vee

Vera,

You are standing between me and the camera.
Please move.

Irene

Zizi,

Can you rush "out front", dear, and tell my son Howard to put his Barbour back on? That fluorescent green tank top is giving _me_ a migraine.

Vee

Tasmin,

Can you rush up to "the box" and have a word with Benjy about the lighting? On my side of the couch, there doesn't appear to be any.

Vee

Tasmin,

Can't you persuade Vera to tone down her make-up in the commercial break? That way, Benjy needn't keep her in the dark. Just a suggestion.

Irene

Ladies!

For God's sake, stop sending me
notes! Just concentrate on trying to do
your job, and let me do mine.

Benjy

Polly!

Can you rush and get me an ice-pack! I was bending down to check my "mark" for my camera position, and Irene poked me in the eye with her clipboard.

Vee

Vera,

My sincere apologies. I <u>swear</u> it was an accident, so there is absolutely <u>no</u> need for retaliatation.

Irene

Irene,

   <u>So</u> sorry my clipboard poked you up the bottom. Everyone in the audience laughed, so at least <u>they</u>'ve got a sense of humour!

   Vera

Girls, girls, girls!

That is absolutely enough! Stop
hitting each other and start talking to
each other – you'll make us a laughing
stock! And may I remind you,
THE PRESS ARE IN!

Benjy

The Shagthorne Gazette

Yesterday's TV
Reviews by Nigel Norris

Two new stars were added to the cable firmament yesterday, in a new magazine programme called *Dales Diaries* (Dales TV, 10.30 a.m.). Those local viewers who are wise (and lucky!) enough to buy their sheep's yoghurt direct from my good friends Howard Small and Antony Flowers at Sheepdipper's Shed (Shooter's Hill, Shale, Shap, Near Great Shagthorne – fabulous wholesale prices negotiable: personal callers welcome) might have recognised the distinctive profile of Howard's mother, Vera Small, joined here by her old chum Irene Spencer. From my privileged position in the studio audience, the two ladies were an absolute delight with their mixture of old wives' tales, joke recipes, hilarious poetry, and comic slapstick – certainly this reviewer hasn't seen anything to match their side-splitting running gag with the clipboard since the good old days of Abbott and Costello!

***** Five star rating – a must see!

irene@thelimes.hethergreen.com

4.45 a.m. in the morning

Dear Christopher,

The other night I e-mailed you, unable to sleep, my mind full of apprehensives about the making of the first "Dales Diaries" cable-television show. Tonight (or rather, this morning) I am e-mailing you, again unable to sleep, but this time flushed with the triumph of success. Yesterday morning we made the show, and it went out live to the whole of Shagthorne and its neighbouring environs, so – to use the vernacular of the "business" – we are well and truly aired!

Naturally Vera was trouble from the word go, right through to the words "it's a wrap" (TV parlance for "home-time"), but, as per usual, I strove to ignore her rudeness and aggression and, apart from a badly bruised bottom, survived intact. Everybody was so giddily intoxicated at having accomplished our maiden opening that the "wrap" party lasted until four this morning! Unfortunately, Vera just can't hold her drink (unlike your good old Mum!), so as per always she made a complete exhibition of herself, dancing on tables, singing ribald songs from the last War, and even, I'm appalled to say, "flashing" various garments of her underwear. A journalist friend of Vera's son Howard, Nigel Norris of the "Shagthorne Gazette", was there for the recording (fortunately he had to leave the party early to get his "copy" in, before Vera "got into her stride"), and though I have not seen his review yet, he left me in no doubt that we would be written up as a "rave".

I am so looking forward to seeing you tomorrow, dear, and though I know you love your motor cars and have been anticipating another long drive out somewhere, cumulating with another exquisite luncheon at a wayside inn, I am rather hoping you will agree to staying with me here at Sheepdipper's Shed instead. Howard and his "partner" Antony are taking some of their sheep to a show (not as audience members – *I* made that mistake! Easily done, if you see the way they spoil their livestock. Heaven knows how they'll behave with their surrogate baby when it is born). No, they're entering the sheep in the "best groomed" category at the Royal Micklechester Agricultural Extravaganza, so they've asked me – albeit at short notice – to "hold the fort" at the farm for the day. Anticipating your customary easy-going attitude, I have been into Great Shagthorne this afternoon and bought some provisions to thoroughly spoil you with some of Mum's home cooking! I hope you won't think that I am "blowing my own trumpet" if I add that I was approached by several members of the public, wreathed in smiles, who wanted to congratulate me on my performance, so perhaps it will be just as well if we do stay indoors – we wouldn't want our lunch to be constantly interrupted by "fans" seeking my autograph. Although, in the long term, I suppose it is just something that I shall have to get used to.

Since I had to walk into the village and back, I couldn't carry any wine. Could you be a dear and bring some with you? You might as well bring a case while you're about it – it'll save my poor old legs. Oh, and a bottle of gin and some tonic. Maybe some amontillado too? And perhaps some brandy if you'd like some. Unless you'd prefer port. Then again, if you want to be able to decide post-pranially what to have with the cheese, you'd better bring both. Or Calvados, of course. Or Sam Bocca? Anyway, I'll leave it up to you.

Can't wait till you get here. Masses of hugs and kisses,

Mummy Irene xxx

vera@dalesdiaries.com

5 a.m.

Dear Howie, Antsh and Tasha,

Too esshited to sleep, so cashing up on mail. Than you so mush for today, can't express how mush I needed your shupport. Eshpeshially getting home from party. Mush do something bout that shlippery shtep. You were all wunnerful at tasting my recipe for "toad in the hole with Sheepdipper's sauce". Hope Tasha is better now. Delishoush though the toad wosh, I did think she was a bit rash having a second helping. An I *know* I shaid "be eye-catching", Howie, but shtripping off and jumping into vat of yoghurt shauce to show iss rejuvnating qualities, wosh beyond call of duty. Dalesh TV have already had sheveral e-mails requeshting your address. Shome have attashed photos.

Now, I may have mish-heard, there was a lot of shouting at the party, but I think you menshioned you and Ants were off to the Micklechesser show thish mornin? If you are thinking of leaving Irene in charge, I can only shay don't! Eshpeshially if there's any of your Sheepdipper's Shardonnnay about. Did you sheee the shtate shee wosh in by the end of the party?

Mush shtop now. Sheem to be sheeing double. Muss be something wrong with screen.

Big kishes,

Mumshie

irene@thelimes.hethergreen.com

5.30 a.m. in the morning

Vera,

Having just "sent" an e-mail to my son
Christopher, I "received" at the same time an e-mail
from you, evidently meant for Howard but
erroniatiously sent to me. I think "pot calling the
kettle" best describes your slanderous accusations
regarding my allegged "inebriation". And as Howard
will be the first to tell you himself, I *never* help myself
to his wine cellar, but keep my own (modest) supplies
in my room.

Since you are quite evidentially not feeling yourself
at this precise moment, I shall turn a blind eye to your
allergations that I am incapable of keeping an eye on
the farm for a few hours in Howard and Antony's stead,
and suggest you go to bed and get some sleep, as I
myself am about to do.

Irene

PS I don't know whether you were "compost mentis"
enough at the party to take in my words of
congratulation on the show but, the clipboard incident

notwithstanding, I thought you managed to take your part quite well.

PPS If you are still feeling poorly on waking, I recommend "Parson's Extra Strength Liver Salts" as a cure. I have never needed to use it myself personally, but I believe from others who have that it is extremely effercateous.

vera@dalesdiaries.com

Saturday 11.00 a.m.

Dear Irene,

Have just come round – thought the terrible banging
was in my head, but it was dear little Sabrina at the
front door wanting breakfast, Karen's still in bed of
course – and after a pot of strong coffee, read your
e-mail. Judging by my state this morning, I must have
been rather "inebriated" myself last night, so I hope
you will take my comments with a pinch of salt.
Parson's Extra Strength Liver Salt, in fact. I'm sure
you're as much in need of it as I am.

I'll refrain from pointing out that I do have a
paragraph at the foot of my e-mails saying they are
confidential and intended solely for the use of the
individual or entity to whom they are addressed. I
can't, however, fault you on obeying the instruction,
"If you have received this e-mail in error, please notify
the sender".

Never mind, my dear, let us put all annoyances
behind us and enjoy our mutual triumph. Have you
read Nigel Norris's piece in the "Shagthorne Gazette"? I
would be jumping for joy if I wasn't feeling so poorly. I
know he is a friend of Howard's, but that counts for

nothing these days. I'm sure he wouldn't have been so eweloginious if he didn't mean it. As for the "clipboard incident", it was obviously such a success I think we should make it a feature. Perhaps we could vary the "slapstick" by tripping each other up with our microphone cables?

To dispel any fear of hard feelings, I shall pop over to Sheepdipper's at lunchtime to make sure you're all right and bring you some of my hangover cure: chicken soup with coriander and sheep's yoghurt. I can't avoid driving through Great Shagthorne, so I shall probably be forced to stop here and there and greet my public.

All 'til later.

Your Fellow Celebrity,

Vera!

Saturday, 12.45 midday

Vera,

Tried to call you, but you must be on your way, so excuse this note left here in haste for you on the kitchen table on the back of this muesli packet – couldn't find any notepaper.

I was just checking my e-mail, and saw yours saying you're coming over for lunch, when Christopher arrived in his Ferrarro. When I agreed to Howard and Antony's tardy request to stay here to look after the farm today, I'd thought that would be all right with Chris, but what I didn't know was that in fact he has a business meeting in Amsterdam this evening, so we've had to hare off to make this afternoon's ferry. Thus, I hope you won't mind milking the sheep in my stead (instructions attached by string to teats in shed).

Natasha is upstairs asleep, as she didn't feel up to going to the show with the boys – she's got a little tummy upset apparently – so she might be able to help you with the muck-spreading if she feels a bit better later. Perhaps you'll be

able to tempt her with the rejunavating
qualities of your coriander soup.

Thanks for helping out. Back tomorrow
evening.

Have fun!

Irene

howard&antony@sheepshag.com

St John!

In haste, am availing myself of Howard's e-mail.
Rang and rang your surgery, but just got "engaged".
You must have a lot of pet emergencies. Can you get
over to Sheepdipper's as soon as you've finished with
them? I'm afraid we have one here. Natasha is rolling
around in agony and I don't think toad in the hole
would produce such a violent reaction.

Vee

howard&antony@sheepshag.com

Irene,

Got here to find the house deserted and screams
coming from upstairs bedroom. Naturally assumed the
worst, i.e. that you had been attacked, ravaged and left
for dead. Even in the sleepy Dales we have our quota
of serial killers. Armed myself with the heritage
ornamental shepherd's staff Howard has mounted on
the wall, and rushed upstairs to find poor Natasha
abandoned and in a terrible state. She told me you had
just left on a "jaunt" with your son Christopher in his
new Focaccio. How could you be so selfish? The poor
little thing was obviously in labour. I couldn't raise the
doctor – Saturday morning, what did I expect? – and
casualty at Micklechester told me an ambulance would
be at least two hours. I rue the day we lost Gt
Shagthorne Cottage hospital! By this time, Natasha
was climbing the walls and I had no choice but to roll
up my sleeves and put on the kettle. Fortunately, my
veterinarian son-in-law St John came to the rescue, still
covered in pig's blood from a tricky amputation.

He got Natasha on to the kitchen table – Howard
won't be pleased about the stains on his stripped pine –
and less than ten minutes later had delivered a perfect
baby girl. Thank goodness there is one member of this

family who is intimate with the parturition process! Fortuitable too, as we all remarked, since he is – biologically, at least – the baby's "father". Natasha made a quick recovery, she's young of course, and in no time we were all sitting in the kitchen – Natasha was still on the table – having a laugh and a large glass of Sheepdipper's Chardonnay. What a pity you missed it.

I do hope the "jaunt" you had with Christopher was worth it.

Vera

Darling Howie,

A quick note on the back of this vaccination reminder card, as I can't find anything else. Welcome home! In your absence you became the happy father of a lovely little girl! I'm proud to say I was the first to hold her in my arms. In fact I caught her as she popped out and shot across the table!

Congratulations, my dear son. And, of course, to Antony.

Your loving Mumsie.

PS Noticed the list you left for the errant Irene. Sorry we didn't have time to do the muck-spreading.

PPS Just heard the sheep bleating. Off to milk them immediately!

irene@thelimes.hethergreen.com

Sunday

Dear Vera,

Here I am, sitting in an hotel bedroom, back in Prague again. Chris has bought me a mobile phone with e-mail facilities (it's called a "Whopper", I believe, which is strange since it is very, very small), and a most marvellous flexible keyboardy thing, which folds up to the size of a cigarette packet, so he can get in touch with me wherever I am, and I can contact anybody, anywhere, anytime! Isn't technology marvellous, once you get used to it?

You may be wondering, Why Prague, I thought she said Amsterdam?, which in fact I did. But Chris loves driving so much that, once his business meeting was over, he jumped behind the wheel of the Ferrarro and before we knew it we were in Checkloslovlaklia. I only hope we make it back in time for rehearsals on Monday but, if not, perhaps you could "improvise" without me for a couple of hours.

Anyway, this is just to say that I got your e-mail about Natasha's birth, and to apologise most profanely. If I had had the remotest inkling the poor girl was in contractions I would not have dreamt of deserting my

post. Please give my good wishes to all concerned –
congratulatory poem to follow.

Sincerely and with love,

Irene

vera@dalesdiaries.com

Monday 7.00 p.m.

Dear Irene,

I wish I could say you were missed at the "Dales Diaries" TV rehearsals this morning but, quite honestly, so much else was going on I don't think anyone noticed. Most of the staff – there are only three as you know – have gone on strike due to lack of pay. I arrived to find complete mayhem which, after a weekend at Sheepdipper's, delivering babies, spreading muck and milking sheep – the poor things were desperate by the time anyone remembered them – was the last thing I needed. Our director Benjy had locked himself in the loo and there were whispers of suicide. Horrified by visions of him drowning himself in the lavatory pan, I dashed to find him. Fortunately, I could still hear sobbing, but I could only entice him out by promising I would spend the rest of the day doing everyone's job for them. I'd already made forty-two cups of coffee by the time he stumbled back to the "studio" with what looked like sugar all over his nostrils.

I've just got home, having drawn up the following programme. We start with me interviewing my son

Howard and his partner Antony about their new arrival and the controversional stir she will cause in Great Shagthorne. Then you perform your congratulatory poem, with backing from the Little Shagthorne Rugby Eleven Cheerleaders (I know there should be fifteen, but they've had a lot of injuries). We'll worry about the rest when you get back. If you do get back. You seem to find your travels in Eastern Europe more fascinating. I almost expect to hear you've got entangled with their notorious Mafia! Come to think of it, it would be fun to interview a gun-runner on the programme. Do get their e-mail addresses if you meet any.

Must hurry up to Sheepdipper's now where my services are, needless to say, indispensable. Natasha will have to go back to her own home soon. As a surrogate mother she is not supposed to "bond" with the baby. Howard and Antony have been in shock since they got back from the Micklechester Show with a first prize rosette and found a baby girl on the kitchen table. As brand new fathers, they don't appear to know one end of the little mite from the other, which is a surprise when you consider how many lambs they have brought up by hand. Perhaps they will feel more at home if they pop her into a sheepskin baby-gro.

For goodness sake let me know when we can expect

your services. If you're not back by tomorrow, I'll have to hire someone else to "front" the cheerleaders.

Vera

PS I presume you *can* twirl a baton?

irene@thelimes.hethergreen.com

Monday 11.00 p.m.

Dear Vera,

Got your e-mail, and I'm so sorry not to have been in touch before about our tardiness in returning. My new "Whopper" phone seems to have had a bug of some sort and I've been unable to make calls or e-mails, but my clever son Christopher has sorted everything out now. He's such a dear boy, and so astonishingly generous, which is why we're delayed of course.

We were enjoying an "al frisco" lunch yesterday outside a restaurant in Prague, when a man who was driving by screeched to a halt and jumped out of his car to admire Chris's lovely red Ferrarro which was parked nearby. Chris strolled over to him, and had soon struck up a friendly conversation. Apparently Ferrarros are very hard to come by in Checkloslovlaklia and its environs, hence the man's excitement, and before I could jump in to restrain my son's generous impulses, he had only gone and swapped cars! Thus we are driving back rather more sedately than we came, travelling as we are in the man's old Skoda, which has already broken down twice. I honestly wonder how Chris manages to make a profit in his Pre-Owned Vehicle Reallocation Consultancy if he is such a soft touch, but he seems utterly undaunted by the deal, and says he is just happy to have made the man's dreams come true!

Anyway, Vera, we are now in Holland waiting for the next ferry, so I should be back for rehearsals tomorrow, albeit rather late. I have, however, written two poems, attached here, so perhaps you will be kind enough to print them off your end, and deliver them appropriately. And do please give Benjy my uttermost apologies for any worry caused.

Best wishes,

Irene

To Howard and Antony, a Child is Born

a poem
by
Irene Spencer

Congratulations Howard,
Felicitations Ant!
For on this day is born to you
A surrogate infant.

I pray that she is healthy,
And beautiful and wise,
And that you two unpractised Dads
Will heed her little cries.

There's the cry she'll make for needing love,
And the cry for needing rest,
A cry for "Change my nappy *now*!"
And in her case, "Where's your breast?"

It's daunting when they first are born,
And you don't know what they mean,
But persevere with patience, dears,
And she'll grow up to be a queen.

For Natasha, Surrogate Mother, In Memory of Services Rendered

by
Irene Spencer

Natasha, dear, your time has come,
  And you must leave the stage,
You've carried your precious cargo well
  For what must seem an age.

You've had your morning sickness,
  And heartburn, and sore back,
So it can't seem fair at the end of that
  For you to get the sack.

No, it must be hard to leave her now,
  But leave her now you must –
And believe me, soon your tears will dry,
  Just like your milky bust.

So, back to "normal" life for you,
  And a return to husband Wayne,
And remember, for Howard and Antony,
  Your loss has been their gain.

Tuesday 11.00 p.m.

Dear Irene,

I gave your excuses to Benjy, with your poems, which sent him straight back to the lavatory. Thinking perhaps it was just the overwrought state he's in, I came up to Sheepdipper's after rehearsals and tried them out on Natasha. She burst into tears, rushed to her room, locked the door and is now refusing to come out or talk to anybody. We've sent for my son-in-law St John, as he is usually the only person able to calm the situation, but I fear all is not well at The Bothy either. This morning as I left for work, I heard raised voices and a terrible crash and had to dodge a pot of marmalade as it came flying through the window.

Where on earth are you, anyway? I know our transport system is in dire straits, but I've never heard of a ferry from Holland taking longer than twenty-four hours. Unless it's gone down with all hands and not so much as an SOS signal.

In case of your continuing absence we've had to get emergency back-up, so I've asked my old friend Yasmin, from my sojourn at Far Shores Trailer Park, to come on the show and do psychic forecasts.

Am going to bunk up here at Sheepdipper's as I'm so tired I can hardly keep my eyes open. Also think I need to be on hand for the baby's night feed. When I arrived, the boys were trying to get milk into her mouth from an eye-dropper.

Vee

The Coach House
The Bothy
Long Lane
Little Shagthorne

Monday

Dearest Yasmin,

I know I've been out of touch for a while, for which I apologise. Do you still specialise in spells, tarot and psychic counselling? If so, how would you like to come and practise them on my cable TV chat-show, "Dales Diaries"? I'm sure you've heard about it. It's been all over the "Shagthorne Gazette".

We've been puzzling over how to improve our "format" and I had a sudden inspiration. "Yasmin and her Tarot"! You're so uncanny with your instant predictions. I'm sure our "audience share" would go shooting up.

Let me know asap, as our next show is this Friday.

All the best,

Vera Small

vera@dalesdiaries.com

Wednesday

Irene,

Don't bother coming back. Yasmin Brown arrived this morning and she is perfect. No fuss about clothes – she always wears the same thing, full Romany costume. She did an absent reading with her tarot cards and said you were "surrounded by swords". So, wherever you are and whatever you're doing, I'm sure you're enjoying it.

Vera

irene@thelimes.hethergreen.com

Dear Vera and Benjy Hartless-Dixon,

I am *so* full of apologia for being away so long that I hardly know where to begin. I have covered half of Europe again since I sent my last communicado, and I'm afraid my "whopper" phone has been on the blink once more so I have been unable to let you know what's been happening. Not that I understand it myself, actually. I really almost fear that Christopher is having some kind of "driving frenzy" breakdown – he hasn't slept for days, being constantly behind the wheel, and he's certainly not behaving like his usual cheerful self. I keep trying to remind him that his Mother has an important job in the media now, and simply must get back to Great Shagthorne with all possible speed – well, I can't fault him on the "all possible speed" part I suppose, we practically broke the sound barrier on the Auto Barns in Germany – but somehow we seem to get no nearer to the Heartlands of England however fast he goes.

We were waiting for the ferry in Holland on Monday night, as you know, and praying that the old banger Chris picked up in Prague would survive the rest of the journey home, when Christopher made *another* new friend who, apparently, had always longed for a Skoda exactly like the one we were driving. This man had an Alfalfa Romeo which Christopher got very excited about, and before you could say, "What *is* it about men and cars?", they had swapped keys and we were getting into the Alfalfa! Of course, Chris was so excited about this new car that he immediately wanted to set off on a test drive, and as we still had an hour or two before the ferry departed I did not demur. Unfortunately I must have dropped off, and when I awoke it was to find that we were almost back in Checkloslovlaklia.

We are now in Prague, I am utterly exhausted, and Chris has just come back to the hotel to tell me that he's swapped the Alfalfa for yet another old Skoda. Honestly, if he's so keen on all this schoolyard swapping, I don't know why he doesn't just stick to Pokeyman cards like your dear little granddaughter Sabrina. Goodness knows when we'll get back – this car looks to be in even worse condition than the last one. Needless to say, I don't think there is the remotest chance of my being there in time for the recording of this week's show, so it is just as well you managed to get Yasmin in to take my place for this episode, even though her predilictions are so wildly inaccurate – I haven't seen a single sword, let alone been surrounded by them – just Skodas, Alfalfas, and Checkloslovlaklians.

Wearily and penitentuarily yours,

Irene

PS Do please tell Yasmin for me to "break a leg".

Thursday

Dear Irene,

Yasmin thanks you, but says she does all her prophecies sitting down. She also warned that you shouldn't take "swords" too literally. Knives and forks perhaps? – what with Christopher's gourmay tastes. Or spanners. It sounds as though you will see a few of those! Your son is obviously car crazy. Perhaps he is a "vehic-aholic"? After all, addictions do run in the family.

To put your mind at rest, the show is going fine without you. We've cut your poetry slot. Yasmin is doing a spell instead. I hope she's going to demonstrate how to turn five-pound notes into fifties! Dales TV is so poor I've had to raid Sabrina's piggy bank to pay this week's bus fares. Benjy is at the hair-tearing stage. The trouble is, he's got no stamina – these "media" types just don't have a balanced diet. In his case, it's far too much sugar. Before we go "on air" on Friday I'm going to make everyone a good, hearty breakfast. Sheepdipper's sausages with stuffed black pudding and devilled kidneys (Yasmin's recipe). It can double as the cookery slot on the programme.

Haven't got time to go into the ups and downs of Bothy life at the moment. I'll just say, frankly, I'm glad to be out all day. When I got back this evening, my grandchildren were sitting on my doorstep with their bags packed. They wanted to say goodbye before they ran away from home.

Hope Christopher's now swapped the Skofa for something more dependable. St John's driving a big green motor which he says is indestructible. I think it's called a Centurian.

All for now dear,

Vera

irene@thelimes.hethergreen.com

Thursday, 1.00 a.m. at night

Dear Vera,

Am finally on ferry. Back in time for tomorrow's recording – hopefully.

Best wishes,

Irene

irene@thelimes.hethergreen.com

Friday 8.30 a.m. in the morning

Vera! Benjy!

Help!! Chris and I are in prison in Hull!!! Please send criminal solicitor to examine our briefs immediately!!!!

Irene!!!!!

c/o Sheepdipper's Shed
Shooter's Hill
Shale
Shap
Near Great Shagthorne

My Very Dearest Christopher,

Words cannot express my utter anguish at being released by the police while you are still languishing in custardy. I simply don't understand why they have continued to detain you for so-called alleged "car theft" when I explained everything to them in my statements about how you had come to innocently swap cars with the gentleman in Prague, and the gentleman in Holland, and then the other gentleman in Prague. I also explained that the reason we had been zipping about between countries over the last few days was simply because you just love driving, and not, as they say, because you were part of a ring of international car thieves dealing in stolen English vehicles. What made me most enraged was the sarcastic laughter my statement was greeted with. How dare they suggest that you used me as a dupe to provide you with the cover of respectability as you went about your criminal ways – when all you ever wanted was to be a good and loving son, and to make up for all those lonely years when society had decreed that we must be apart.

Believe me, I didn't want to leave Hull when you were still imprisoned there, but, as the solicitor pointed out, I can be of most help to you now if I keep calm and put all my efforts into trying to get you free. Hence I have come back to Great Shagthorne and taken up my role again as co-presenter on "Dales Diaries", in order to use the "power of the media" to prove your innocence. This week's show is going to be almost entirely devoted to you, my darling son – I shall be telling your tale of false accusation in epic poem form, and announcing a twenty-four-hour phone line where people can ring up with any information that might help us get to the bottom of this. And Yasmin the psychic Romany will be trying, telepathetically, to discover the truth behind this sorry tale. I don't know what Vera is planning yet, as she seems to have her hands full with her daughter Karen at the moment, who's taken the birth of her new niece very hard – but then I always warned she would. No young woman could be expected to be over the moon about the fact that her husband had secretly "performed" with a stranger who had been hired to rent out her feminine accoutrements by said young woman's own brother, in order that he and his gay "partner" may continue the family line. Needless to say, Vera takes Howard's part in all this and has no time for poor Karen – she is a fool where her blessed son is concerned, and in her opinion the boy can never do wrong. However, you have your own troubles at the moment, and don't need to be bothered with this.

Try not to worry, although it's easier said than done – we'll soon have you out of prison and your innocence established. And though it is true that I had to give you up when you were a little baby, never, for one moment, dear, fear that I will ever abandon you again.

Your loving Mummy Irene xxx

Dear Irene,

Yasmin told me you propose to hijack the "Dales Dairies" to campaign against the so-called "injustice" suffered by your son. She was mortified when she realised I knew nothing of your plans – she may have second sight, but she often can't see what's under her nose. She is now pouring over her tarot cards, trying to find a solution. When I mentioned the idea to our director Benjy he went quite white. Come to think of it, he was white already, or at least his nose was, he had just come out of the lavatory – odd for a man to powder his nose, but then, we are in the "entertainment industry".

I'm afraid he doesn't feel the Dales TV audience is "ready" for this sort of provocative material and it might frighten the horses. Or in the Dales case, sheep. I pointed out that he had employed us – well me, anyway – to be original, to which his only reply was, "Not that original."

Of course I sympathise. What mother wouldn't? I know how hard it is to discover that your child has a mendacious and criminal nature. Goodness knows it took me long enough to accept it about Karen. But face the facts, Irene. It's obvious your son has been up to no good. It can probably be put down to the many years he spent without nurture. How much, really, do you know about his background? Was he "in care" for example? Or saddled with abusive step-parents?

I have no objection to your telling the sorry tale of having to abandon him and this life of crime being the result. Even Benjy agrees that would be "good television". But we really don't have the resources to rival "Crimewatch"! Sending the solicitor to get you out of prison and study your briefs has already cost more than we had in the kitty. I've had to ask St John for a loan.

The best I can offer is that I persuade Benjy to let you make an appeal for funds at the end of the programme.

Yours,

Vera

PS Tasmin's just e-mailed me a "funky" idea. How about a live link-up with the prison cell and then Chris can tell his own story? Do find out if he's willing.

irene@thelimes.hethergreen.com

Dear Vera,

Speaking of "mendacious and criminal natures", how on earth did you think you could get away with trying to pull the wool over my eyes about what Benjy thinks? Do you suppose I do not have my own, extremely good, relationship with our producer? Although then again perhaps you do not regard him as such – your last e-mail "*I* have no objection; the best *I* can offer" etc., makes it sound as if *you* think *you* are performing that role.

In fact, it was Benjy himself who came to me with the idea of making this episode of "Dales Diaries" all about Christopher. He, at least, seems to believe in my son's innocence. The reason, most probably, that he went white when you spoke to him about it, is because he knew you would make a fuss, wanting as you always do to be the focus of the limelight. Well, Vera, you have already had your turn with having your son on the programme, and now it's mine. Yes, all right, perhaps Christopher's story of false imprisonment will be more newsworthy than Howard's inability to sire his own child, but that's the way it goes sometimes – I certainly didn't arrange it on purpose! Nor, while we are airing our differences, did I arrange for all the fan-mail about my poetry in the first episode to be sent to the production office, or indeed the letters of disappointment Benjy received after the second programme when I didn't appear, demanding that my poetry slot be reinstated.

As for the money you say *you* spent on the solicitor, may I be so bold as to remind you that you do not run the budget? For if you did, you would know that I have already paid it back in full. Haven't you noticed the money Christopher lavishes on me? Do you really suppose he cannot pay his own way, and that he will not reimburse me every penny?

I cannot spend more time on this "storm in a teacup" as I am working on my *Magnus Opus* for this week's episode. If you don't want to be party to the theme of this programme, perhaps you should take a week off? I'm sure your daughter Karen could do with your full attention just now, suffering as she is from the shock of being made, simultaneously, both step-mother and aunt. Then again, if you cannot bring yourself not to be in the public eye for a week, I suggest you just go your own way and do one of your recipes. I believe a couple of people did write in to say they liked them.

Best wishes,

Irene

PS Benjy and I have already applied to the prison governor for a "live link-up" and had our request denied, so Tasmin, as per usual, is way behind the times with her "funky ideas".

PPS CHRISTOPHER THOROGOOD IS INNOCENT!!!

Benjy!

I've just had the most extraordinary e-mail from Irene, claiming that you and she have entered into a conspiracy behind my back to devote the whole programme to her good-for nothing son Christopher. What on earth are you up to? When I suggested you should let her make an appeal after her no doubt excremental "epic poem", you said, if I recall, "Over my dead body." What changed your mind? Or whom?

If "Dales Diaries" must submit to the embarrassment of another ton of insulting e-mail, at least have the good manners to warn me in advance! And what's all this about the legal-fee money being repaid? It certainly hasn't made it to my bank account, nor indeed to that of my son-in-law St John.

Answers before tomorrow's rehearsal, please!

Vera

benjy@dalestv.com

Vera,

For Christ's sake calm down! After you and I spoke, Irene rang me in floods of tears, threatening to kill herself. Even worse, on the programme. I don't think the Derby Dales can cope with "Snuff TV". Do you? The two of you piss me off so much with your idiotic squabbles, I really don't care any more. It's making me ill. In fact so ill, I've got to stop and go to the lavatory.

Later:

Feel a bit better, now. Look. We both know Irene's under a lot of stress at the moment. Why not humour her? Don't forget we are chasing ratings. Audiences are suckers for people in captivity, if the success of Big Brother-type shows are anything to go by. Can't you dream up a recipe for prison gruel or something?

Benjy,

PS 'Fraid the money got recycled. I had to apply a lot of pressure to the prison governor for the live link-up. It obviously wasn't enough.

vera@dalesdiaries.com

Dear Benjy

Very well. To please you. We can't have you collapsing on us. One nervous breakdown per programme is quite enough! I will just warn you though that Irene tries this ploy quite often.

Fortunately I do have a prison recipe. An unpleasant memory from my own days "inside". But that was in a former life, a long time ago, and I won't go into it now. Whatever you've heard about it from Irene is bound to be pure fabrication, and anyway, she can talk. She was released on grounds of insanity.

Vee

Prison Gruel
Porridge oats
Salt
Water

One bucket porridge oats to two buckets of water and a pound of salt. Put in a cauldron and heat ferociously. Serve with large lumps in.

irene@thelimes.hethergreen.com

Dear Benjy,

Here, as promised, is my Appeal For Information in Epic Poem form. Have you hired the extra staff to deal with the response yet?

Best wishes,

Irene

Mishaps and Misunderstandings

an Epic Ode
by
Irene Spencer

Coincidences do happen,
And lightning can strike twice,
For there are more things in heaven and earth,
Than are dreamt by men and mice.

For instance, see that young girl,
A-pregnant with her first –
School uniform a-straining,
Its seams all fit to burst?

(I should point out right here and now
This wasn't her intention –
She was set upon by a ghastly man
In an act too crude to mention.)

Imagine now that babe when born
Is torn from t'young maid's side,
And they wouldn't tell her where it went,
No matter how she cried.

Could ever Mum find babe again,
Could ever babe find Mum,
In a spinning world as large as ours
In a search till kingdom come?

"Of course not!" Comes the cry from you,
"It's a needle in a haystack!"
But I'm here to tell you, forty years on,
That Mum did get her babe back.

He sought her here, he sought her there,
He followed her all over –
For no man loved a woman more,
Except p'raps Casanova.

She had not named him "Chris", it's true,
When first she'd kissed his neck,
In fact she'd called him Gregory
After her hero Mr Peck.

Nor had she called him Thorogood,
When like her, he'd been born Onions,
But what's in a name? Would not roses smell sweet,
With the nomenclature "Dandelions"?

A joyous year thus then ensued,
Beyond this bless'd reunion,

Twelve months of love and tenderness,
Of happiest communion!

The babe, a man now, took his Mum,
On drives both near and far,
For second place in his heart next her,
Was his love for the motor car.

Forty years he had to make up,
For their cruel separation,
And thus, by driving her to Prague
He sought to make reparation.

And now we come back to coincidence,
And lightning striking twice,
For he swapped his car on the way back home
Not once, but in fact thrice.

It wasn't the act of a criminal,
Despite police suspicion,
It was the kindly act of a charitable man,
Of a generous disposition.

For the men he swapped with envied him
His motor cars a lot,
And with my son, if you say, "That's nice,"
He'll give you all he's got.

But do the police believe his tale
Of philanthropy gone wrong?
No – they keep him in a jail in Hull,
Pray God, though, not for long.

Thus, this is why I need your help,
And why I now appeal,
For information you may have,
Of men you know who steal.

Search high, search low, I beg of you,
Send hounds throughout the nation –
For to set him free I must prove a case,
Of mistaken identification.

howard&antony@sheepshag.com

Mumsie darling!

Ants thinks he knows a man, who knows a man, who knows a man, who knows Irene's son Christopher. This chap – a right old tart, by the way – recognised Chris's photo when it flashed on to the screen during Irene's appeal for info, and said when *she* knew him, he was in Pentonville and was known as Clifford "The Noye" Thomson. Apparently, Cliffie was inside for pirating Norman Wisdom videos. Has he got a heart with "Mum" written in it, tattooed on his left buttock? If so, it's definitely him.

Irene moved into Shagthorne's Queen's Hotel yesterday. She told your Dales TV producer darling Benjy she'd just got to have her own "crisis-control centre". Must say it's a relief – I don't want to think what our telephone bill will be! Don't know how she will take this news, so will leave it to you to tell her.

Meanwhile, where on earth have you been? It's all very well being a B-list celebrity, but what about the cost to your own family? Mumsie we *need* you at Sheepdipper's. It's all gone *horribly* pear-shaped! Our baby-mother Natasha is refusing to leave. She says she has changed her mind about giving up the baby. She's been phoning St John's emergency bleeper at all hours of the day and night, as if there's anything *he* can do about it! Yesterday, my dear sister Karen descended in a towering rage. Natasha snatched the baby and locked herself in her room and Karen all but broke the door down. Ants had to restrain her with the sheep-shearing harness.

We still haven't even agreed on a *name* for our little girl! Ants and I have had frightful rows over it. We came to blows – the first time ever! – over Tiger Lily versus Heavenly Hiraani. We're temporarily calling her Small Flowers, which at least has an oriental ring about it.

Do, *please* forget about "Dales Diaries" for a *nano*-second. Your nearest and dearest are feeling *very* neglected!

Howie

vera@dalesdiaries.com

Dear Irene,

Is the Gt Shagthorne Queen's Hotel comfortable? I
do hope so, as it's five-star and putting you up there,
with constant access to your own information hotline,
fax and e-mail, has taken what remains of our budget.

Amongst the welter of malicious and prank
e-mails – I believe it's called "spam", I can't think why,
it isn't pink, though it's often slimy – I received in
response to your "appeal" was one from my son
Howard. He and his partner Antony have an
acquaintance who swears he can identify your son. I
know it's a delicate question, but have you ever seen
Christopher in his underpants?

Vee

PS Don't let anxiety drive you to raid the mini-bar.
Dales TV can't afford it.

irene@queensgreatshag.co.uk

Dear Vera,

Yes, thank you, I am quite comfortable here at the hotel (please note temporary new e-mail address). I had to move out of Sheepdipper's Shed because of the violent rows which were occurring due to the surrogate-baby situation of your son Howard and his partner Antony. Not only were they screaming and throwing things at each other at all times of the day and night, but also the baby's mother Natasha is of a – shall we say "fevered" personality. Add to this your daughter Karen's obvious distress about her own husband St John's part in all this baby-making activity, and I am sure you will appreciate that staying with Howard at this particular moment in time was quite untenantable, particularly given my own current anxieties about getting my son Christopher out of jail.

A propose of Chris, I hardly think it likely that he would know *anybody* of Howard and Antony's acquaintance, either in or out of his underpants. However, leads are coming in from elsewhere, thanks to last week's show. Several people have e-mailed suggesting an uncanny resemblance between Christopher and a Clifford Thomson, who is a known criminal, and I have apprised the solicitor of this for inclusion in Chris's briefs.

No time for more now – too many e-mails to reply to. See you at rehearsals tomorrow.

Best wishes,

Irene

<u>vera@dalesdiaries.com</u>

Dear Irene,

I can assure you that I wasn't being "personal" when I asked for Christopher's intimate details. Now others have apprised you of his likeness to the criminal Clifford Thomson, I can reveal that he is precisely the person Howard and Antony's friend claims to know. The proof lies in his underpants. Or if you prefer, his "briefs". To put it bluntly, does he have a tattoo on his bottom? If you can't bring yourself to look, here is another clue. Does he have a particular fondness for Norman Wisdom videos?

Heaven knows I am the last person to enjoy being the bearer of bad tidings, particularly to an old friend, but I'm afraid, Irene, that yet again you have fallen victim to your allusions. Do be careful, my dear. We all know how charming a villain can be – look at the legends inspired by the Kray twins – but in Pentonville, Christopher was notorious for his psychopathic leanings.

As for your concern about Karen and co, I can assure you that none of it is news to me. For the last week my modest coach house has been host to all the children, as well as Natasha in tears, St John in despair and Karen setting fire to the curtains. She claims it was her cigarette, but I *know* it wasn't an accident.

If you want to get me before rehearsals tomorrow, e-mail me at Sheepdipper's. Howard has just arrived in the cheese van and is begging me to rush up there to sort everything out. Really, families! I'm beginning to think we should *all* be given away at birth.

With love and sympathy for your endeavours – however misguided,

Vera

irene@queensgreatshag.co.uk

Vera,

Talking of "misguided", don't you see that what you have just divulged to me a propose of tattooed buttocks, is not proof of Christopher's guilt but, "au contrary", his innocence! Presumably the police at Hull mistook Chris for this Clifford Thomson person, since they are apparently so uncannily alike, and now all they have to do to clear the whole matter up is to look at his bottom, see for themselves that it is unblemished by art work, and set Chris free.

I have e-mailed the solicitor this new relevation, and eagerly await his response. Do thank Howard and Antony for me, from the *bottom* of my heart. Pun intended!

Gaily and relievedly yours,

Irene

PS Have you had any ideas for this week's programme? I'm afraid I've been so wrapped up in my own troubles I haven't even cast a thought in that direction. Let's do something upbeat – I'm in the mood for joy!

<u>howard&antony@sheepshag.com</u>

Dear Irene,

How about a programme devoted to the "joy" of Prozac?

Vera

<u>irene@queensgreatshag.co.uk</u>

Dear Vera,

Having scurfed the Web to find out what "Prozac" is, I have discovered that it is an antidepressant, and thus imagine you were attempting a poor joke when you wrote of its "joys". Ha ha.

While you were thus engaged in ribaldry, your daughter Karen arrived here in a terrible state, saying that she has left her husband St John because he is in love with Natasha, her brother's surrogate baby-maker. She says she has tried to talk to you about it but, as always, your sympathies lie entirely with your family's male members.

I hope you check your e-mail while having a fun, "joy-filled" time over at your son's farm, so that you may come here to the Queen's Hotel immediately thereafter to tend to your distraught and tragically "joyless" daughter. Or perhaps you would like *me* to be Karen's "surrogate" mother?

Irately yours,

Irene

PS That was a rhetortical question, Vera, so don't even think of trying to be clever or amusing. Just get here.

Dear Irene,

I wasn't "trying to be clever or amusing", I was absolutely serious. As recommended by Benjy – whom, it turns out, has been on Prozac since the day we started "Dales Diaries" – I took a few of his prescription pills to Sheepdipper's with me. Without mentioning a word to anybody, I ground them up and put them in the cocoa. The effect was like a miracle. Especially on me. Everybody became perfectly calm and listened while I told them what they should do. Life is so much more pleasant when no one is arguing and shouting, don't you think? I'll pop up to Great Shag. Queen's in a jiffy and bring some for you and Karen. I'm just going to top up everyone's cocoa and wait for them to fall asleep. According to Benjy it takes about fifteen minutes.

Vee

Vera,

Two hours have elapsed since you last mailed, so I can only assume you have fallen asleep yourself while "telling everybody what they should do". Really! The lengths you will go to to get your own way. Fortunately, Karen is asleep now too, aided and abetted by my old-fashioned drug-free sleep remedy, three parts whisky and one part hot water.

I myself personally am quite unable to join you all in the Land of Nod, since I have just received some very upsetting and mystifying e-mails, which I am forwarding to you for your circumspection. What shall I do? What does it all mean? Nothing's as it seems, it seems. And where's the blithering room service when you want them to restock your mini-bar?

Distraughtedly yours,

Irene

loveridge@sidebottom&associates-solicitors.com

Dear Mrs Spencer,

With reference to your last communication to this office, it is with regret that I write now to inform you that the man you have regarded as your son Christopher Thorogood is in fact Clifford Thomson, also known as Cliff The Car, Thompson The Tealeaf and Tommy The Gun.

Since you are no longer related to the criminal in question, may I assume that you will no longer be requiring the services of this firm? I await your further instructions.

Yours,

Malcolm Loveridge

<u>evie@nuff-said.co.uk</u>

Deer Missus Spencer,

I wotched your tv program abaht my nipper, Cliff. Where do you get orf sayin he's yores? Forty-two weeks I carried that kid, and I've got the stretch marks to proove it. Leeve us allone. We've got enuff on as it is.

Yvonne Thomson (Mrs)

howard&antony@sheepshag.com

So sorry, Irene! Dropped off. Odd, as I didn't put any pills in my cocoa. There must have been a mix-up as I was refilling Howard's mug. He'd chucked his first lot over Antony.

What a shock these e-mails are! But I'm afraid it's only what I, as your friend, have been trying to warn you of. Is it possible that Christopher is still your son, as well as all these other nomdee-plooms? Perhaps "Yvonne Thomson" has her own reasons for claiming to be his mother. She may be allusional? Or the keeper of the swag, under her patio? I don't know which is worse, to be the foolish victim of a hoax or the mother of a notoriously murderous criminal. Irene, you may have had a lucky escape!

I'm coming to hold your hand – or head, if you've emptied the mini-bar – as soon as I can get a taxi and, in the absence of drink, I shall bring calming medication. According to Benjy, it can take a while for it to "kick in", so I'll also bring a bottle of Sheepdipper's Chardonnay.

All my love,

Vee

<u>irene@queensgreatshag.co.uk</u>

Dera Vera,

Tahnks droppin in with wine. You're goo girl when your goo. Noboddy has better pal than you when your nice. Lovely. Karen still out like light. Goin join her.

See you rehersles tomorrow.

Big hug ol frend,

Irene

Dear Vera,

Woke up with terrible headache, now made even worse by attached missive, which appeared in my e-mail "Inbox" this a.m. What is happening to my life? I seem to have lost one son and gained another – or is the entire male prison population playing at chain letters with me?

Help!

Irene

HMP GREYTOWERS

Dear Mother,

It feels strange to write that after so long a search for you. And it will be even stranger for you to read it, I imagine, since you currently believe your son to be the Christopher Thorogood who is also known as Clifford Thomson, aka a hundred other aliases.

In fact, he shared my cell for a few months when he was last inside, and I foolishly confided in him that I was looking for my lost mother. There is only so much research one can accomplish here in prison, and when it came time for Cliff (or Chris if you prefer) to leave, he offered to follow up my latest lead – I had discovered an Irene Spencer, née Onions, living in Hethergreen. The rest, as you know, is history. He found you, and impersonated me in order to use you as an alibi while he drove stolen cars to Eastern Europe – he's a very incompetent villain, I'm afraid. (I think that he also believed you must be rich, if I was taking so much trouble to find you.)

A friend saw your television show and gave me your

address. I had hoped to write to you for the first time when I was on the outside, not from my prison cell. What must you think of me?

I will not trouble you further if you prefer, but – please, Mother – may I dare to hope that you will allow me to explain?

Your only true son,

Christopher Thorogood BSc (OU)
Prisoner M354176

C/o The Queen's Hotel
Great Shagthorne

Dear Prisoner M354176,

I am sorry, but I cannot bring myself to call you "Christopher" yet, without incontraveneous proof of your identity. You will understand, I am sure, that I have spent some months bonding with He Whom I Thought To Be My Son, only to find that I have been lied to and used as an alibi for criminal pursuits, so now I am a tougher nut to crack maternal-feelings-wise.

Do, by all means, write to me to offer further proof of why you believe me to be your Mother, but – and I hope you will excuse my inquisition – also please explain why you are in prison. Call me narrow-minded if you will, but I am afraid there are some crimes that I would find completely unpalatable in any son of mine.

Yours sincerely,

Irene Spencer

vera@dalesdiaries.com

Dear Irene,

Thank you for mailing me the copy of your letter to "Christopher Two". I can't help feeling it's a little starchy though. I know you are feeling daft and wounded, but it's not his fault someone decided to prey upon your gullible and self-deluding emotions by impersonating him. He may be in prison for some mere misdemeanor, after all, he *is* a BSE. Consider the close brushes with the law other members of your family have had – I won't forget, for example, you being arrested for head-butting a bulldozer.

I think the best idea would be for you to go and visit him. This time accompanied by me. I would provide an empartial and judiciacal opinion of the situation and then you'd be much safer. What's more, having failed (thank goodness!) to achieve our last "live link-up", we should cover this first meeting in a "Dales Diaries" show. I've run the idea past Benjy and he agrees that, whichever way it goes, it would make "terrific television". Viewers love tear-jerking scenes or, indeed, shouting, swearing and threats of

violence, if the popularity of soap operas is
anything to go by. We haven't yet decided on a theme
for this week's show, so we'll discuss it at rehearsals
later.

Love,

Vee

Darling Mumsie,

Thanks *so* much for coming to look after us. Your cocoa was fab – I had no idea it could be so calming. When Ants popped my orange dazzle and ginseng tea by my side this morning, I felt like the sleeping beauty being woken by my prince after a hundred years slumber. Even our baby-mother Natasha has stopped screaming. In fact, she's stopped doing everything – except for wandering around like a zombie, bumping into the furniture. I only hope she will see sense now, and return to her rightful home without baby Small Flowers. Or baby-father St John.

I'll mail you later with an update. Meanwhile will get on with the chores while I'm so light-hearted and *gay*!

Howie

irene@queensgreatshag.co.uk

Dear Vera,

Thank you *so* much for taking time out of your hectic schedule to advise me on how to manage my affairs with the person in prison who claims to be my son. I am afraid I will have to decline your kind offer to accompany me to visit him with the "Dales Diaries" camera crew in tow, however. Your errant son-in-law St John turned up here at my suite at the Queen's at six a.m. this morning, banging on my door, demanding to be let in. I persuaded your daughter Karen to see him and hear him out, which she finally agreed to after much shouting, and they were just starting to see eye-to-eye again when who should start shoulder-ramming the door but Natasha the surrogate baby-maker . . .

Can't write more now – am needing to keep a sharp look-out for flying missiles. Get here as soon as you can and sort your warring family out – the management are complaining about the screaming.

Irene

<u>irene@queensgreatshag.co.uk</u>

Dear Benjy,

Grab a camera crew and get over to the Queen's Hotel fast. There's a spurned mistress here in a cat-fight with the jealous wife, refereed by the husband.

Irene

Benjy, Darling,

Ignore Irene's last. I'm over at the Queen's now and I
have thrilling news! I have persuaded my daughter
Karen, her husband St John, my son Howard, his
partner Antony and their "baby hostess", Natasha –
you remember them all, I'm sure, from your
documentary "A Life With Sheep" – to appear on our
next "Dales Diaries" show. As you know, ever since
Natasha became pregnant by the somewhat
unorthodox method of using my son-in-law, St John, as
her "sperm donor", our family has been experiencing
typical "modern-life" problems. Karen has left home,
Natasha has gone mad – I wonder now about those
pills you gave me – St John has a black eye, a sprained
wrist and a fractured skull. Howard and Antony are
having nervous breakdowns over the potential loss of
their surrogate daughter Small Flowers, my
granddaughter Sabrina has been arrested for holding
up the Bangladeshi owner of our paper shop with a
home-made cheese straw, and my other two
grandchildren, Nelson and Millie, are both wetting the
bed. Thinking about that, though, I suppose they
might be anyway, as they're only a year and a half and
six months respectively.

A few people (Irene, for example) may think we shouldn't bare all in public, especially on a pre-waterfall show, but exposing ourselves on TV will, we all agree, be a wonderful catharter. Also a wonderful boost to our audience share – Jerry Springer, eat your heart out!

I will get the entire family into the studio at 10.00 a.m. tomorrow, and may the best man, woman, (or child) win!

So pleased and excited!

Vera

PS Reply to me at home rather than above address, which is that of the Queen's Great Shag manager.

benjy@dalestv.co.uk

Vera,

Unless we get funds from somewhere immediately, this will be our last show. May as well go out with a bang. Besides I'm too exhausted to argue.

Yours,

Benjy

irene@queensgreatshag.co.uk

Dear Benjy,

Since this – the last ever episode of "Dales Diaries", I am led to believe – has evidentially become "The Vera Small Show", I assume I am "de trope", which is fine by me.

I am checking out of the Queen's Hotel today to spare you further expenditure, and can be contacted, should you need me, on my old e-mail address of: "irene@thelimes.hethergreen.com", which I can access from wherever I prove to be.

Thank you for some jolly times.

Best wishes,

Irene Spencer

benjy@dalestv.co.uk

For Christ's sake, Irene, get a grip! I've never worked with such unprofessionals – and that includes the sheep. If you don't turn up for the show tomorrow you'll never work in this town again. Well, in these Dales anyway!

Vera! What on earth have you said to Irene now? She's threatening to just take off and abandon the last show. I don't believe you two! Can't you, just for once, bury your selfish differences for the greater good – i.e. moi? I wish to God I'd taken my father's advice and become a ballet dancer.

Right. Either you get Irene back, or I'm downing earphones this minute. There will be no "last show". Your barking-mad family will never get air-time anywhere else. Come to that, nor will you. So. Think about it!

vera@dalesdiaries.com

Benjy,

Have you been at the sugar again? I think you must be allergic! It's the same problem with my grandson Nelson. He goes potty after a tube of Smarties. Believe me, Irene is just, in your parlance, "winding you up". She couldn't bear to miss out on a drama like this one!

Vee

vera@dalesdiaries.com

Dearest Irene,

I've just received the most disturbing e-mail from
Benjy. The poor boy is obviously deranged. He seems to
think you would abandon old friends and loved ones in
their moment of greatest need. You – and only you –
know how indispensable you are both to the show and
our well-being in general. There is no way my tragic
children and grandchildren could go through the ordeal
of trial by TV without the knowledge that you are
standing in the wings (metaphoristically speaking) with
a comforting smile and an even more comforting glass of
alcohol. To say nothing of how bereft I would feel, dear
friend, if you were no longer by my side – that is, slightly
behind me and to the left – to shoulder the burden of
public adulation. I have told Benjy not to be a noodle – I
worry about his medication – I hope I know you better
than that! But, just to put his mind at rest, do be an angel
and e-mail him that of course you will be appearing. I'm
aware you couldn't bear to be left out, and who knows
what tomorrow may bring in terms of revelation!

Your oldest best friend,

Vera

Dear Vera,

Picked up your e-mail on the "whopper" phone that He Who Claimed To Be My Son bought me. Am currently on a train back to Hethergreen, waiting in a siding while some "wrong type of leaves" are cleared from the track.

It was not my intention to "abandon old friends" in a cruel-hearted way – I was merely missing my home and thinking that you and your family problems could easily fill an hour's television without any help from me. This TV-star, hotel-living lifestyle is all very well, but, to be honest, I do feel the absence of the normal round of Bring and Buys and Keep Fit Classes and ordinary honest-to-goodness village life that used to fill my days.

However, since you all evidentially feel that the show cannot go on without me, I shall get off at the next stop and do a U-turn. If no return train is available I will hire a mini-cab. Warn Benjy to have enough cash to pay the driver when I arrive, and to re-book my suite at the Queen's.

Best wishes,

Irene

Henry Moore Ward
Micklechester Infirmary
7.00 p.m.

Dear Irene,

Just dropped by to leave you some flowers, but the
nurse said you were asleep so I'm penning this quick
apology on your hospital notes. (I see you're off the
"critical" list, thank goodness!). Words can't express
how sorry I am – we all are – about the turn events
took this morning. Nobody, not even our resident
psychic Yasmin, expected Natasha's husband Wayne to
turn up out of the blue and come storming into the
studio. Apparently, being a night worker, he watches a
lot of daytime telly and is a big fan of "Dales Diaries".
Unfortunately Benjy, for bona fida marketing reasons,
had put out a rather inflammatory trailer – Natasha in
her underwear etc. etc.

As Wayne explained later, when he leapt in front of
the cameras, grabbed the coffee table and splintered it
over your head, he was actually aiming at St John. In the
ensuing scrum there were quite a few other injuries.
Karen sustained a broken nose (from Natasha), Natasha
a black eye (from Karen), Antony a kick in the crotch
(from Howard) and Howard fainted. Poor boy – he
never could stand the sight of blood. What a good job St

John had brought along his emergency veterinarian first-aid kit. He had some animal tranquilliser he'd prepared earlier and Benjy was the first to avail himself of it. Even I did not escape unharmed. I was so hoarse from shouting over the mayhem, I had to consume an entire packet of "Good Girl" doggie cough drops.

Thank heavens you were there to witness the scene – at least until you were knocked-out cold. Otherwise I don't think anyone (except the viewers) would believe me! The good news is our ratings have gone shooting up and, as a result, several people have come forward offering financial rescue packages. Edward Blunt – remember him? Our chicken farmer suitor? – is willing to plough in "seed" cash (I hope that doesn't mean *bird* seed) in return for Blunt Farms product placement. Benjy is doubtful, saying it's morally wrong to accept money from dubious sources, but I can't see the harm if it just means using his chickens and eggs. None of my recipes specify they *can't* be genetically modified.

Must hurry home now, to sort out everyone and feed them. The way things are going, it may well turn into the last supper!

Get well very soon, my dear. As you say, we can't do without you.

Vera XX

Henry Moore Ward etc.

Dear Vera,

Woke up a couple of hours ago thinking I was in a greenhouse! The nurse tells me that all the flowers are from you – as if I needed telling. For a person named Small, you have always been one for the large gesture. Anyway, thank you for the thought.

I think, though, that the lesson to be learned from all this is that, in future, once I make my mind up to do something I shall do it, despite any exaltations from you to the contrary. I don't know why, but I had a definite feeling in my waters that something awful might happen to me if I stayed in Great Shagthorne.

I have to agree with Benjy about not wanting to get involved with Edward Blunt again. He is a person of dubious character and, personally, I wouldn't trust one of his cocks as far as I could throw it – which isn't far at the moment, what with the lesions in my neck . . .

Later:

Honestly! As if I hadn't had enough "family reunions" for one day! I take it I have *you* to thank for alerting Prisoner M354176 (also known as "Christopher Thorogood", or He Who Thinks He Is

My Son) to my current condition. The hospital social worker has just been to see me, and told me that the criminal in question has got a temporary compassionate discharge, and is heading this way!

Yours in agony and in terror,

Irene

Henry Moore Ward
Micklechester Infirmary

My Dearest, Only True Son, Christopher,

How wonderful at last to have found you!
(Although, of course, I have a strong sense of jardez-
vous when I write that, given my experiences with
your imposter, that reprobational recinivist Clifford
Thomson.) As soon as I saw you walking towards my
hospital bed I knew in my heart that you were mine,
albeit that you were handcuffed to a prison officer.

So strong was my sense of recognition of your looks
and mannerisms, I didn't need the extra proof of you
showing me your birth mark – the dusky tincture of
which I had last seen a lifetime ago when I had kissed
it tenderly through tears of anguish at our enforced
separation. I am glad that your adoptive parents treated
you, for the most part, kindly, and so sorry that you
have been cruelly accused of a crime you did not really
commit. You are right, of course, when you say that
your naivety blinded you to what was going on but,
speaking for myself, I would rather have "naive" than
"knowing" as a personality trait in any son of mine.
You are quite wrong, however, to think that you are
less dashing than the other "Christopher" – I always
thought that his strawberry-blond locks looked rather

effeminate on a man. Anyway, baldness is meant to connote manliness, isn't it? Look at Yul Brynner, or Sean Connery without his toupee. And if I had been asked at the time of your birth to choose International Car Theft or Accountancy as a career for you, I would have chosen Accountancy every time.

My dear, I am so glad that you will soon be released from your long ordeal, and that I may see you again, unfettered and free. I intend, as soon as I am discharged from hospital, to return home to Hethergreen, where I look forward to welcoming you to your true family home.

With all the love that I have been longing to lavish on you ever since you burst asunder from my loins.

Your loving Mother,

Irene xx

PS I am sorry your visit was interrupted by Vera's unannounced arrival. She is a long-time friend, and very nice in her way, but prone to "drama" and giddy outbursts of inappropriate hilarity, I am afraid.

vera@dalesdiaries.com

Dearest Irene,

I'm so glad I dropped by with that Sheepdipper's special frozen bilberry yoghurt whip. Otherwise I might not have met "Christopher Two" for years! How happy I am for you, dear friend, that you have at last found the true fruit of your enforced and unhappy union. I'd have known him anywhere, even in his prison uniform and handcuffs. In fact, now you have met the real one, you must be asking yourself how you could ever have been taken in by the obvious falsity of "Christopher One"? But remind yourself, he put himself out to disassemble, with his manners, charm and attractiveness – unlike Christopher Two who is much more "oh naturell". Including his hair – or lack of it! Much more, in fact, like you.

I know, with your strongly disapproving nature, you will be giving yourself sleepless nights over Christopher Two's "crime". My advice is, don't. Cooking the books is nothing nowadays, it's almost de riguwer if you're an accountant. I only wish my own nearest and dearest would give me so little to worry about. We got through the weekend narrowly avoiding arson, murder and infanticide. And that was just from my granddaughter Sabrina, who is clearly feeling in need of attention. I won't burden you with the details when you're poorly, but it was like something out of a bad novel. In fact, after all this, I should be writing one! Ah, Irene, I too feel a nostalgia for our simpler, more "normal" lives. Jamming, pickling, doing the church flowers – it all seems so long ago . . .

Oh, that reminds me, as local celebrities we've been asked to open the new "organic" extension at Tesco. I've explained that you are feeling the need to be "ordinary" at the moment, so they've begged me to do it alone.

Must dash to Shagthorne Shearers now, to get my hair done. I'll pop in tomorrow, afterwards.

Big hug,

Vera

<u>irene@queensgreatshag.co.uk</u>

Dear Vera,

I am sorry that you were so obviously put out by my surprise appearance at the Organic Celebrity Opening at the supermarket – doubly so, since I had thought that you would be pleased to see me back on my feet so soon after being attacked by a member of your "extended family". Your fears that I would frighten away the shoppers with my neck brace and facial lesions were entirely unfounded judging by all the autographs I was asked to give – and I don't know if you've seen today's "Shagthorne Gazette" yet, but as the front page headline is "The Show Must Go On – TV Star Bravely Battles Bruises To Be With Her Fans", I rather imagine that the bulk of Great Shagthorne's population was happy to see me make the effort to fulfill my obligations, even if you weren't.

I have come back to the Queen's Hotel to pack my bags and rest for the night before returning home to Hethergreen, but I'm wondering what to do with the things your daughter Karen has left in my room. Elton, the hotel manager, tells me that Karen continued to stay here while I was in hospital, but that she left this morning with a man and they haven't seen her since. Any clues up your end?

Before closing, I must correct you on a couple of points. My son Christopher did *not* knowingly "cook the books" – he merely signed chits for various items purchased by his firm without being, in retrospection, absolutely 101 per cent sure what they were, and if said items actually existed. Nobody was more surprised than he when the police stormed into his office in bulletproof vests, waving guns, and arrested him for fraud. He has a very good idea which board members were the actual culprits, but as one is a Lord and the other a Sir, naturally they have got off scott-free and with ne'ery a finger pointed in their direction. So much for the "classless society" we hear so much about these days.

If I don't hear back from you before I check out of the Queen's, I shall leave Karen's things in a carrier bag at reception. I can't wait to be home in my own bed! I just hope that Beryl-next-door has managed to do my plant watering while I've been away – she's got bladder problems now, as well as her ongoing bottom saga, did I tell you?

All best wishes for a speedy return to "normality", whatever your interestingly different family think that is.

Irene

vera@dalesdiaries.com

Dear Irene,

By the time you get this, you will be at home
tucked up in your own little narrow bed – I recall
thinking, last time I visited, that I really couldn't bear
to live in such a tiny flat. There's no room to swing a
cat, so it's just as well you haven't got one of those for
Beryl-next-door to water! Talking of which, do give
her my condolences on her other watering problems.
She seemed such a nice woman when I met her, but
then I've never had to deal, face to face, with her
bottom.

I hope you found everything as you left it, which is
so reassuring when for a brief span one has been
inhabiting "another world", i.e. that of a busy and
thoroughly fulfilled person. Speaking for myself, I've
been inundated with requests for further appearances,
since the spread in the "Shagthorne Gazette". I don't
know whether you read beyond your own mention,
but it went on to say that as a home-grown star of
Dales TV, I'd done everything in my power to put the
Shagthornes on the map. They've now become a
heritage tourist attraction and a "Vera's Tea-shop"
franchise is being proposed for the villages. There were
some lovely snaps of me on pages three, four, five, six

and seven. There was *one* of you, and I don't think the neck brace and facial scars were *too* unbecoming.

Thank you for packing up Karen's things, which St John has now collected. The man with whom Karen left was, it turns out, Natasha's husband Wayne. Needless to say, St John and Natasha are both devastated. Of course, as the abandoned partners, it is hardly surprising that Karen and Wayne "bonded" – though I have an idea that Wayne's strapping good looks and blond ponytail had something to do with it. I fear Karen will never change. We have not yet been apprised of their whereabouts, or intentions.

In the meantime I must get on and cook supper right now. Sabrina will be home from school any minute and I've got Nelson in his playpen, Millie in her bouncer and Small Flowers in her crib to attend to. I'll worry about the so-called "grown-ups" later!

Do keep me up to date on life in Hethergreen. It will be a relief to hear of the dull old day-to-day routines.

All for now, dear,

Vera

irene@thelimes.hethergreen.com

Vera!

I imagine your phone line is busy because you are putting the police on full alert, but don't bother. I had just finished unpacking my cases when Sabrina turned up, having hitch-hiked here all on her own. She says that her mother has abandoned her, and that her Granny Small is too busy with "other people's children" – by which, I gather, she means her half-brother Nelson, her half-sister Little Millie, and her half-stepsister/surrogate-cousin Small Flowers – so she's come to live with Granny Spencer.

What do you want me to do? Obviously she can stay here for a while, but as you rather pointedly said in your last, my flat *is* on the compact side, so I think I shall have to decline her kind offer to adopt me. The poor little mite. She's feeling so unwanted and unloved. Hasn't Karen phoned you yet to tell you where she is?

Got to go – Sabrina's calling for her cocoa.

Irene

Dear Irene,

Thank you for letting me know you have got Sabrina. To be honest, I didn't know she'd gone. She often threatens to run away when things get too much for her, but this is the first time she's actually done it. I imagine it's to do with the trouble she is in at home. I was indeed on the phone to the police – apparently a gang from Sabrina's school has been running what the CID man calls a "credit card scam" and they suspect Sabrina of being the ringleader. If you have any cards I advise you to hide them.

So, Irene, it looks as though you are harbouring yet another criminal. At this rate we will soon *both* be visiting relatives detained at her Majesty's pleasure! I'll drive up and collect her tomorrow.

Yours, emotionally drained,

Vee

PS Not a word from Karen and Wayne. I've now got Yasmin and her crystal ball on to it.

Dear Vera,

"Tomorrow" has come and gone with neither sight nor sound of you, which has only confirmed poor little Sabrina's opinion that "nobody cares" . . .

Later:

Well really, what next! I paused there to investigate the frantic sounds of disturbance from my back passage, expecting it to be you turning up late, only to discover it was Karen! She had no idea Sabrina was here – she just couldn't think where else to go when Wayne dumped her on the side of the motorway while they were having a row.

Will you and St John *please* come here AT ONCE and sort this sorry mess out. As fond as I am of your family, my own son Christopher has written to me with his imminent release date from prison, and I need the space.

Best wishes,

Irene

Dear Irene,

Sorry! More trouble with baby-mother Natasha.
St John caught her about to try to slash her wrists.
He had to drag her to the veterinary surgery and apply
his famous gaffer tape. The fuss she was making,
screaming it was all his fault she'd "lost Wayne", I said
he should put another piece over her mouth – really,
I'm at the end of my tether!

We'll definitely be there by tea-time.

Vee

Dearest Irene,

Frightful journey back to The Bothy. Karen shouting, Sabrina crying, St John swerving all over the road! We arrived to find Natasha had left with Wayne. After dumping Karen, he had driven straight back to collect his estranged wife. She'd scrawled a note saying she never wanted to see any of us again. She and Wayne are going to try for their own baby and she gives up all rights to Small Flowers. Howard and Antony are so relieved. I suggested, at once, they employ a full-time nanny. That way the other grandchildren will get my full attention. DI Malton thinks, in view of the "home circumstances", Sabrina will get away with a caution. I must say though, her credit card activity has given me a great idea on how to revive the "Dales Diaries". Nothing illegal, of course!

We all celebrated with Sheepdipper's Chardonnay, and I noticed, after the third bottle, Karen and St John disappeared, holding hands. So, All's Well That Ends Well – as the Bard said. We shall just have to see, won't we?

Love, as always,

Vera

irene@thelimes.hethergreen.com

Dear Vera,

Astonishing news! Not only is Chris being released sooner than expected, but he has also just informed me that he is married with two children! I'm a Granny and a Mother-in-law again in one fell swoop! He's invited me to join them at their home next weekend for his Coming-out Party, and has very sweetly extended the invitation to you too, as my friend. Do, please, *try* to behave yourself, if that isn't too much to ask . . .

See you there.

Your happy friend,

Irene

PS Don't feel obliged to go into detail about Sabrina's brush with the law, or Karen's cat-fight or Natasha's suicide attempt – I'm sure Christopher had more than enough of the seamier side of life when he was erroniatiously incarcerated. Try to keep the conversation light and upbeat.

PPS It is to be an informal, family affair, I am told, so

you can leave your backless fishtail taffeta at home. Personally I shall be wearing something warm and comfortable in a neutral shade.

Dear Irene,

Really, as if I would in ANY way set out to embarrass or discombobulate you! What do you take me for? Not only will I not mention any of the above, but neither will I refer to your daughter Lesley's bizarre marital arrangements or, indeed, to your own time "inside". Though, come to think of it, that might make him feel more "at home".

For the record, I shall be wearing my new cerise cashmere two-piece and a gorgeous little peacock-blue cocktail hat, with one or two feathers.

Very much looking forward to making Chris and his family's acquaintance.

Vera

PS And, as ever, to seeing you.

LADIES OF LETTERS.COM

Carole Hayman and Lou Wakefield

Ladies of Letters.com – the third series of the hilarious Radio 4 show, and Vera and Irene's correspondence is as coruscating as ever . . .

Dear Irene, Can't bear for you to fly halfway round the world in violent outrage. It would only give you flatulence and nothing is worse on a cramped plane. I've enclosed a photo of us which is one of my favourites. It was taken in Capri by a gentleman who invited me to the casino . . .

Dear Vera, I remember the gigolo incident very well. You claimed you had 'forgotten' to take your spectacles out with you, so did not see the hourly rates written on the back of what you cared to think of as the gentleman in question's calling card . . .

Dear Irene, I hope you've settled in and are over your jet lag, which must have been considerable if you drank Bloody Marys all the way. I can imagine what a killer feeling lonely and unwanted can be, but you're not falling back into your old habits, are you . . . ?

Dear Vera, Once more I shall gloss over your illusions to my so-called drinking habit. Honestly, talk about the pot calling the kettle! You may have chosen to forget who it was who had seventeen 'Long Slow Screws' in Majorca . . .

YOU CAN READ ME LIKE A BOOK

Maureen Lipman

'Od's blood, this book doth make a man
besmirch himself with merriment'
Ben Jonson

Ms Lipman's homogenized life has skimmed through headlines like 'Maureen Goes Bonkers in *Yonkers*' and 'Maureen is *Gorgeous* at last', to an unscheduled appearance in another kind of theatre from which she emerged with considerably less than she had when she went in.

Read how she gained a cricket team and lost her place in *Outside Edge*. How she became Enid Blyton at work and an outsized chicken at home, how she found her way into directing and ended up, via the kitchen sink, in *Agony Again*. Along the way Ms Lipman is unshutdownable on topics such as Supermodels, Sleeping Policemen, Cones, Cohens and Critics; she wards off Awards, salutes Streisand and snuggles down with something with a hard spine. See her quaking in Los Angeles, barking in the Chinese Year of the Dog and contemplating matricide by the seaside.

Fancy it? Oh well, please yourself . . . Better still, let her do it for you. Start on page one – you can read her like a book.

Other bestselling Time Warner Paperback titles available by mail: